D1120455

# Spreading It Around

# Londos D'Arrigo

A SAMUEL FRENCH ACTING EDITION

SAMUEL FRENCH
FOUNDED 1830

SAMUELFRENCH.COM
SAMUELFRENCH-LONDON.CO.UK

Copyright © 2014 by Londos D'Arrigo
All Rights Reserved

*SPREADING IT AROUND* is fully protected under the copyright laws of the United States of America, the British Commonwealth, including Canada, and all other countries of the Copyright Union. All rights, including professional and amateur stage productions, recitation, lecturing, public reading, motion picture, radio broadcasting, television and the rights of translation into foreign languages are strictly reserved.

ISBN 978-0-573-70253-2

www.SamuelFrench.com
www.SamuelFrench-London.co.uk

### FOR PRODUCTION ENQUIRIES

#### UNITED STATES AND CANADA
Info@SamuelFrench.com
1-866-598-8449

#### UNITED KINGDOM AND EUROPE
Plays@SamuelFrench-London.co.uk
020-7255-4302

Each title is subject to availability from Samuel French, depending upon country of performance. Please be aware that *SPREADING IT AROUND* may not be licensed by Samuel French in your territory. Professional and amateur producers should contact the nearest Samuel French office or licensing partner to verify availability.

CAUTION: Professional and amateur producers are hereby warned that *SPREADING IT AROUND* is subject to a licensing fee. Publication of this play(s) does not imply availability for performance. Both amateurs and professionals considering a production are strongly advised to apply to Samuel French before starting rehearsals, advertising, or booking a theatre. A licensing fee must be paid whether the title(s) is presented for charity or gain and whether or not admission is charged. Professional/Stock licensing fees are quoted upon application to Samuel French.

No one shall make any changes in this title(s) for the purpose of production. No part of this book may be reproduced, stored in a retrieval system, or transmitted in any form, by any means, now known or yet to be invented, including mechanical, electronic, photocopying, recording, videotaping, or otherwise, without the prior written permission of the publisher. No one shall upload this title(s), or part of this title(s), to any social media websites.

For all enquiries regarding motion picture, television, and other media rights, please contact Samuel French.

R0443289841

## MUSIC USE NOTE

Licensees are solely responsible for obtaining formal written permission from copyright owners to use copyrighted music in the performance of this play and are strongly cautioned to do so. If no such permission is obtained by the licensee, then the licensee must use only original music that the licensee owns and controls. Licensees are solely responsible and liable for all music clearances and shall indemnify the copyright owners of the play(s) and their licensing agent, Samuel French, against any costs, expenses, losses and liabilities arising from the use of music by licensees. Please contact the appropriate music licensing authority in your territory for the rights to any incidental music.

## IMPORTANT BILLING AND CREDIT REQUIREMENTS

If you have obtained performance rights to this title, please refer to your licensing agreement for important billing and credit requirements.

*SPREADING IT AROUND* was first produced by the Stage Door Players in Atlanta, Georgia on January 23, 2009. The performance was directed by Robert Egizio, with set design by Chuck Welcome, costume design by Jim Alford, lighting design by John David Williams, sound design by Dan Bauman, and wig design by George Deavours. The Production Stage Manager was Courtney Loner. The cast was as follows:

**ANGIE DRAYTON** . . . . . . . . . . . . . . . . . . . . . . . . . . . . . . . . . Holly Stevenson

**MARTIN WHEELER** . . . . . . . . . . . . . . . . . . . . . . . . . . . . . . . .Brink Miller

**LARRY DRAYTON** . . . . . . . . . . . . . . . . . . . . . . . . . . . . . . . . . .Jacob York

**TRACI DRAYTON** . . . . . . . . . . . . . . . . . . . . . . . . . . . . . . . . Amanda Cucher

**DR. KRAPINSKY** . . . . . . . . . . . . . . . . . . . . . . . . . . . . . . . . . . . Larry Davis

# CHARACTERS

**ANGIE DRAYTON** – Likeable, caring, active woman in her late 60s.

**MARTIN WHEELER** – A fit, well-preserved man in his early 70s.

**LARRY DRAYTON** – Angie's son. An arrogant, self-important fellow in his mid-30s.

**TRACI DRAYTON** – Larry's wife, and Angie's daughter-in-law. A self-absorbed fashionista in her mid-30s.

**DR. KRAPINSKY** – A serious man in his mid-50s.

# SETTING

The living room of an upscale home in a gated community in Florida.

# TIME

Present-Day

# ACT ONE

## Scene One

*(Setting: The living room of an upscale home in a gated community in Florida. The decor is casual but expensive. Along with the usual furnishings of sofa, easy chairs, coffee table, etc., there is a desk with a cordless phone on it. The front door opens into the living room. On opposite side of room a swinging door leads to the kitchen. Along back wall a hallway leads to the bedrooms. There is a lanai with sliding doors opening onto a terrace which overlooks a golf course. In the lanai is a lounge chair and beside it a large, potted palm.)*

*(At rise: the room is empty on a sunny Florida morning. **ANGIE DRAYTON** enters through front door. **ANGIE** is a likeable, caring, active woman in her late sixties. She is sportily dressed in an outfit appropriate for a woman of her age and means. She drops her purse onto sofa. She goes over to desk, picks up a piece of paper and reads.)*

**ANGIE.** *(to herself)* "Milly Fantuzzi."

*(She checks name off with pen.)*

*(satisfied)*

There. All my ladies accounted for. *(She suddenly droops with fatigue. She looks at her watch.)* Only ten in the morning and I'm exhausted.

*(She goes over and plops onto sofa. She lies with her eyes closed a few moments. **MARTIN WHEELER** enters house through lanai and comes into living room. He is a fit, well-preserved man in his early seventies.*

7

*However, he moves listlessly and is shabbily dressed. He has on gardening gloves and carries a large pair of hedge clippers. As he heads towards front door he drops clippers.)*

**MARTIN**. Damn!!

*(ANGIE jumps up, frightened. MARTIN is just as startled as she is.)*

**ANGIE**. Oh my GOD!! *(She sees it is MARTIN and is relieved.)* Oh it's only you Martin. You frightened the life out of me!

**MARTIN**. YOU?! You scared the bejesus out of ME!

**ANGIE**. *(clutching her chest)* Even in a gated community like this, a woman alone can't help but be a little jumpy. *(She straightens her clothing.)* After what I've just been through, a fright like that was the last thing I needed.

**MARTIN**. Why? What happened?

**ANGIE**. I had to rush Milly to the hospital. *(admiringly)* Eighty-five if she's a day, but there's no stopping that woman. Anyhow, every morning, like clockwork, I check-up on all the widows here in the complex. Someone has to. We're down here in sunny Florida while our kids are hundreds of miles away. Even if they did call once in a blue moon, if something went wrong, what help would they be?

**MARTIN**. Could you speed it up, Angie? I'm not getting any younger. I'd like to live to hear the end of this while I'm still above ground.

**ANGIE**. *(hurriedly)* Well, I kept calling Milly but there was no answer. So I raced over to see what was the matter.

**MARTIN**. *(impatiently)* And?

**ANGIE**. She'd fallen off a ladder. Painting her ceiling.

**MARTIN**. A ladder? Everyone knows after sixty you don't even dare stand on a phone book!

**ANGIE**. It was so sad. The poor dear kept saying, "Please God, don't let me die! Please God, don't let me die! I just bought a new pair of shoes!"

(**MARTIN** *picks up hedge clippers.*)

What are you doing with those? *(teasing)* Wait! Don't tell me. I can see the headline now. "Mild Mannered Neighbor Attacks Extremely Attractive Widow With Hedge Clippers!"

**MARTIN.** *(not amused)* For your information, I was out back pruning your bougainvillea. Nearly got myself killed.

**ANGIE.** *(lightly)* Really? Twenty-four hour security around this place and you were mugged by a climbing vine?!

**MARTIN.** Very funny, Angie. But no, it was those blasted golfers. I had to keep dodging their balls. I swear they were deliberately trying to hit me. No one's slice can be THAT bad. Not even Howard Ditmeyer's.

**ANGIE.** Well you have to expect that, Martin. Our houses back right onto a golf course. Maybe if you played, you'd feel differently.

**MARTIN.** *(grumpily)* You won't catch me spending my days out in that scorching sun, hitting some stupid ball around.

**ANGIE.** Then why did you buy here? They didn't just slip the course in when you weren't looking.

**MARTIN.** *(irked)* Because Peggy fell in love with the house. She wanted it, so we bought it. Then she up and dies on me. Leaves me spending my days in a house I don't want to be in because it reminds me of her. And to top it all off, I'm now forced to look out at a bunch of geezers wearing lime green pants and pink shirts. *(annoyed)* All they talk about are their handicaps. Wearing those get-ups, they've got a handicap alright. They're color blind.

**ANGIE.** *(concerned)* Martin, I'd like to discuss something with you.

**MARTIN.** Oh?

(**ANGIE** *gestures for him to sit.*)

**ANGIE.** Have a seat.

(**MARTIN** *sits on sofa.* **ANGIE** *sits in chair across from him.*)

**ANGIE.** (*hesitantly*) I... I don't quite know how to put this. It's difficult to say.

**MARTIN.** (*matter-of-factly*) Which usually means it's going to be difficult to hear. But go ahead, spit it out.

**ANGIE.** Alright, here goes. I realize it's only what, two months, since Peggy died?

**MARTIN.** (*solemnly*) It'll be seven weeks, tomorrow.

**ANGIE.** I know you're going through a difficult time. You're in mourning. But, well, I'm concerned about the changes I've seen in you. Starting with the way you look.

**MARTIN.** (*defensively*) What's wrong with the way I...?

**ANGIE.** (*cutting him off*) When Peggy was alive you always took such pride in your appearance. Only now, well frankly, you've really let yourself go. Just look at those pants. And that shirt! The pocket is ripped and...

**MARTIN.** (*cutting her off; irritated*) Well excuse me. I knew this was an exclusive community, but I didn't realize there was a dress code to do gardening.

**ANGIE.** Oh dear, I hoped you wouldn't take this the wrong way.

**MARTIN.** Someone tells you you look like a bum, there's a right way to take it?

**ANGIE.** (*sighing*) You're certainly not making this easy. (*She takes a deep breath.*) But here goes. I also want to say I'm concerned about how depressed and negative you've become.

**MARTIN.** (*fiercely*) What do you expect me to do? Cartwheels with firecrackers shooting out my...?

**ANGIE.** (*cutting him off*) Now Martin, no need to be crude! (*patiently*) Of course not. I understand perfectly. I realize this is all a phase in your grieving process.

**MARTIN.** A phase? Acne is a phase. That you grow out of. What I'm going through is old age. THAT you DON'T grow out of! What's life all about anyhow? Huh? You get to be my age, sickness and death are just looming everywhere. If you do manage to wake up in the morning – the rest of the day is like looking down the barrel of a gun.

*(He gets up and heads towards front door.)*

**ANGIE**. Where are you going?

**MARTIN**. *(angry)* I'm taking my shabby ass and the black cloud that hangs over my head back next door where it belongs.

*(**ANGIE** is upset. She gets up and takes his arm to stop him.)*

**ANGIE**. *(soothingly)* Oh Martin, please stay. I was just trying to help. How about a cup of coffee? I promise not to say another word about it. I will keep my big mouth shut. *(imploring)* Please. Say yes.

**MARTIN**. *(grudgingly)* Well, okay.

**ANGIE**. *(relieved)* Good. Now sit.

*(**ANGIE** points to sofa. He goes over and sits while she heads towards kitchen door. She tries to cheer him up.)*

You know that isn't true, don't you? About it being over for you. Why where would I be if it weren't for all the repairs you do around here?

**MARTIN**. *(dismissively)* Yeah, sure, so now the meaning of life is fixing a leaky toilet. *(thawing somewhat)* What happened to that coffee you promised?

**ANGIE**. Oh, right. There's some left in the pot. I'm afraid it's been sitting around for ages. I'll just go heat it up in the microwave.

*(**ANGIE** goes into kitchen. **MARTIN** takes off his gardening gloves. He self consciously looks down at his clothing and attempts to rub some of the stains off his pants and flatten the creases in his shirt with his hands. **ANGIE** comes out of kitchen holding a coffee mug with a Happy Face on it. She hands it to **MARTIN**.)*

**ANGIE**. There you go.

*(She sits in chair across from him while he takes a sip. He grimaces.)*

**MARTIN**. Whew. This is bad. Even for you.

**ANGIE**. I'm sorry. Let me make you a fresh cup.

*(**ANGIE** gets up to take mug. **MARTIN** pulls it away from her.)*

**MARTIN**. No, it's fine. I appreciate you not going to any trouble.

*(**ANGIE** sits back down.)*

**ANGIE**. I said I was sorry. No need for sarcasm.

**MARTIN**. No, I really mean it. Thanks for not turning a cup of coffee into a big, overblown production. That's why I don't mind coming over here. You don't fuss over me like all the other widows do.

**ANGIE**. Oh?

**MARTIN**. Don't tell me you haven't noticed! They're all over me like a…a sweater in a half-price sale. Trying to seduce me with their homemaking skills.

**ANGIE**. Oh Martin, you're exaggerating.

**MARTIN**. The hell I am. They're nothing but a pack of vultures. And they've been circling me since Peggy died. Like I'm a prime piece of roadkill. Some of 'em even before she passed. They had the nerve to show up at the hospital with casseroles. Then they'd invite themselves back to my place to 'heat it up!' What did they expect? With my wife lying there dying – I was suddenly going to ravish them over their Eggplant Parmesan?

**ANGIE**. They're all just trying to be kind. They realize you've suffered a loss and …

**MARTIN**. *(cutting her off)* Horsefeathers!! All that domestic one-upmanship is their way of trapping me. *(disdainfully)* Why any one of them would have served this in a fancy, little cup. *(He holds his pinkie finger up.)*

Then kept plying me with cookies on a dainty plate with a doily on it. *(grimacing at the thought)* And then there's always the dreaded, itsy bitsy, flowered napkin.

**ANGIE.** *(laughing)* You don't have to tell me. I've been to luncheons where Martha Stewart would feel as out of place as a stevedore.

**MARTIN.** Damned relief to be here where you don't give a hoot about serving god-awful coffee in a mug with a Happy Face.

**ANGIE.** *(archly)* Well excuse me. They were all out of ones with a frown!

*(softening)* But, if I'm not mistaken, there was a compliment in there somewhere, wasn't there?

**MARTIN.** *(grudgingly)* I guess so. *(hesitantly)* So, uh, now that we're talking personal, mind if I ask you something?

**ANGIE.** *(taken aback)* Well, uh, no. Just as long as it isn't my age or natural hair color!

**MARTIN.** How come you aren't trying get your hooks into me? Like every other widow within a hundred mile radius. *(sheepishly)* Not that I think I'm so hot. But, it seems anything in pants with a pulse turns them on.

**ANGIE.** Actually, from what I hear, the biggest turn on is a man who can drive at night.

**MARTIN.** *(pressing her)* Well, what's the matter, aren't I good enough for you?

**ANGIE.** *(laughing)* Of course you are. Only for your information, Martin Wheeler, I'm not looking for a man. You or anyone else.

**MARTIN.** *(brightening)* Hallelujah.

**ANGIE.** *(teasing)* No need to sound so thankful.

*(**ANGIE** gets up and paces.)*

It's just that I'm not like those women. I don't need a man in my life to make it complete. That's one of the advantages of not having had a particularly happy marriage. I learned early on how to cope on my own. My Jerry was a workaholic.

He was never around. I basically raised the kids all by myself. I got used to doing everything without him. When I think about it, I realize I was a widow the entire time I was married. God knows I'd loved to have had a wonderful marriage. Like you and Peggy. I envied the way you were always doing things together. How you enjoyed one another's company so much.

**MARTIN.** *(simply)* When she died, I lost my best friend.

*(**ANGIE** goes over and sits across from him on sofa. She pats his hand comfortingly.)*

**ANGIE.** I know she was, Martin. I miss her too. Nowhere near as much as you, naturally. Only that's exactly what I'm talking about. While Jerry was a good man, we hardly even knew one another. When I'd ask how his day had been, he'd always answer, "Same old, same old." Then he retired, we moved down here and three weeks later he dropped dead. *(jokingly)* Sometimes I think he did it just to avoid having to make conversation with me. *(seriously)* But now, the one thing I'm actually grateful to him for is making me independent. Not like so many of my women friends who are left not even being able to balance a checkbook. So, there. No need to worry about me trying to snare you. As far as I'm concerned we are simply two next door neighbors fortunate enough to get along very well together. Nothing more.

*(**MARTIN** gets up and sets his mug down.)*

**MARTIN.** Well, that's a load off my mind. *(He goes over to desk.)* You mentioned one of your desk drawers was stuck.

*(**ANGIE** rises, goes over to desk and attempts to pull out top drawer. It won't open.)*

**ANGIE.** Yes, this one.

*(**MARTIN** tugs at it and it finally opens.)*

**MARTIN**. There! Just needs a little sanding. It's all this Florida humidity. I don't know what it's harder on. The furniture or my arthritis. *(He holds his leg in pain. He heads towards front door, picking up garden clippers as he goes.)* I'll just get some sandpaper. Be back in a minute.

*(**MARTIN** exits through front door. **ANGIE** picks up his mug and takes it into kitchen. She reappears moments later carrying a metal coffee filter and a small garden spade. She heads towards lanai. **MARTIN** enters through lanai holding a piece of sandpaper. He almost bumps into her, frightening her.)*

**ANGIE**. MARTIN!! You scared the daylights out of me. Again!! Why on earth are you coming in through the lanai?

**MARTIN**. That pain in the ass Hancock woman was coming down the street.

**ANGIE**. Vivian. So?

**MARTIN**. She's the worst of the lot. Comes on like gangbusters, that one. Hugging and kissing me like we're long lost lovers. Not to mention the way she dresses. Or should I say, doesn't dress. Wearing her tops down to here and her shorts up to here. *(He indicates a low top and a high short.)* She looks like something out of a "Grannies Gone Wild" video.

**ANGIE**. *(admonishingly)* Now Martin, that's not very kind.

**MARTIN**. Well it's the truth! She looks like a floozy! But I guess she has to, to make up for her lousy cooking. *(He shudders.)*

She made me a meatloaf that was so bad, I'll lay odds that's what killed her husband. *(He notices coffee filter and spade she carries.)* What are you doing with those?

**ANGIE**. Promise you won't tell anyone? I'm sure the complex has a bylaw against it. *(She lowers her voice, conspiratorially.)* I bury my used coffee grounds around the orange tree out back. To fertilize it.

**MARTIN**. So that's why it smells like a Starbucks out there. Well, your secret is safe with me. *(He holds up sandpaper.)* I'd better get started on that drawer.

**ANGIE**. And I'd better get rid of these.

(**MARTIN** *goes over to desk. He takes drawer out and begins sanding edges.* **ANGIE** *exits through lanai. She returns carrying emptied coffee filter and spade and goes into kitchen. She comes out of kitchen empty handed.*)

Sometimes I don't even know why I bother.

**MARTIN**. With what?

**ANGIE**. I had such hopes when I planted that tree. Only it's been nothing but a disappointment.

**MARTIN**. Really?

**ANGIE**. Yes. I haven't had a single orange off of it. *(She sighs.)* My dream was for my grandkids to step out the door of their grandma's house and pick one. I thought it would be a wonderful memory for them to have. *(sadly)* Only they've never even been down here to visit. Not once.

**MARTIN**. That's a shame.

**ANGIE**. Yes. Breaks my heart. *(hotly)* However they did manage to get to Disney World last year. Their parents obviously felt throwing up on Space Mountain was more important than visiting their grandma.

**MARTIN**. Aw, they're all the same. My son was down for Peg's funeral. Once it was over, he couldn't get away fast enough. Haven't heard from him since.

**ANGIE**. *(resignedly)* Oh well, what can you expect? They've better things to do than spend time with us old folks. *(irked)* Although sometimes I can't help wondering whether the walls around this complex are there to keep out the thieves and murderers — or our kids! *(cheerfully)* But just wait! One day I'll have oranges on that tree, and when I do, you and I will enjoy them.

**MARTIN**. That's right. We'll show 'em.

**ANGIE**. And they'll make the perfect breakfast drink.

**MARTIN**. Oh?

**ANGIE**. Yes. We'll get our Vitamin C and caffeine – all in one glass.

*(They both laugh.)*

*(lights dim)*

## Scene Two

*(Lights rise on ANGIE's living room a few days later. There is a laptop computer on desk. ANGIE is in middle of room doing Tai Chi – badly. She waves her arms, stretches and bends – looking frustrated the entire time.)*

*(phone rings)*

ANGIE. *(to herself)* Not a minute too soon! *(She goes over and answers phone. Into phone; tensely.)* Hello. … Oh hi, Betty. … No, nothing's wrong. I was just practicing my Tai Chi. … That's how you broke your collar bone! Goodness, what happened?… You tripped over your coffee table after you moved all your furniture around for good luck. *(She looks puzzled, then something occurs to her.)* Oh no Betty, that's not Tai Chi – that's Feng Shui.

*(MARTIN comes out of kitchen carrying his toolbox. ANGIE doesn't notice him. He goes over to thermostat on wall, takes cover off and begins adjusting it with a screwdriver while she talks.)*

…You'll pick me up at seven for our computer class. That's perfect. I'll see you then. Bye. *(She hangs up. She sees MARTIN and is taken aback.)* Oh my Lord, Martin! There you go again startling me. I thought you were in the kitchen fixing the toaster.

MARTIN. I was. Now I'm tuning-up the air conditioner.

ANGIE. But you just tuned it up a week ago. There's nothing wrong with the air conditioner.

MARTIN. *(matter-of-factly)* Exactly. Because I keep tuning it up.

*(ANGIE looks exasperated.)*

What's this about a computer class?

ANGIE. Pardon?

MARTIN. Just now. You said something about a computer class.

**ANGIE.** Yes. I'm taking one so I can learn how to use the laptop I just bought.

**MARTIN.** What'd you go do that for?

**ANGIE.** So I can get with the times. *(sheepishly)* The other day, Heather, from three doors down, told me she had a blog. I said, "That sounds painful. Have you seen a doctor?" She laughed, then explained what it was. I was mortified.

**MARTIN.** Well, when you unplug it, just don't go pulling it out of the outlet by the cord.

*(He goes back to fiddling with the thermostat. ANGIE is fuming. She tries to control herself but can no longer hold back.)*

**ANGIE.** Martin, I think it's time we had a little talk.

**MARTIN.** Another one? *(sarcastically)* Don't tell me. You think I should wear a tie to clean your gutters. Right?

**ANGIE.** Don't be ridiculous. It's just that, well, you seem to forget this is my house.

**MARTIN.** *(irked)* I built a company from the ground up. I'm not an idiot. So?

**ANGIE.** Every time I turn around, you're there. With your toolbox. It's as if my life has become one very long episode of "This Old House." I don't want to sound ungrateful, but honestly, I don't have any privacy anymore.

**MARTIN.** Well, if I am, it's because I'm fixing your screens. Or the cord on the toaster that you keep….

**ANGIE.** *(cutting him off; angrily)* Would you just keep quiet about that! Now, if you would just let me finish.

**MARTIN.** *(folding his arms; defensively)* Go ahead.

**ANGIE.** Thank you. For example, take the other morning. I walked out of the shower and you were standing in the middle of my bedroom. There I was, wringing wet, with nothing but a towel around me and…

**MARTIN.** *(defensively)* I was checking out the ceiling fan. You told me the squeaking was keeping you awake nights. I wasn't trying to catch you in the....

*(ANGIE modestly clutches the top of her blouse.)*

**ANGIE.** *(cutting him off; mortified)* Good gracious. That's not what I was getting at. It's just that, well, I'm not used to having someone around. ALL the time.

**MARTIN.** *(hurt)* I didn't realize I was getting on your nerves.

**ANGIE.** All I am trying to say is you really have to find something to do with your life – besides fix-it chores around here. There has to be something more productive and worthwhile you can do.

**MARTIN.** At my age? Are you kidding? I've just been kicked aside. Put on the shelf. I'm relegated to being nothing more than a handyman. Which, from the sounds of it, I've just been fired from. So I'll finish this up and head back to my place and get out of your hair! For good!

**ANGIE.** Now Martin, you've over-reacting. I was just trying to …

*(frustrated)* Oh, forget it!

*(MARTIN returns to working on thermostat. ANGIE is exasperated. She resumes her Tai Chi position.)*

*(muttering to herself)*

Cantankerous old… *(trying to collect her thoughts)* Now where was I? Oh yes.

*(She waves her hands as she crosses through room.)*

**MARTIN.** Hold it! I just remembered something.

*(ANGIE stops in her tracks, her concentration broken.)*

**ANGIE.** *(seething)* Now what?

*(MARTIN takes an envelope from his shirt pocket.)*

**MARTIN.** That numbskull mailman left this in my box. I guess postie is another job I'm overqualified for – since I can read!

(**ANGIE** *goes over and takes letter from him.*)

**ANGIE.** *(coolly)* Thank you. *(She looks at envelope, surprised.)* A letter. All I ever get are bills. *(She opens envelope and takes out a letter. A small photo falls out. She picks it up.)* And there's a picture.

*(She reads letter while **MARTIN** continues fiddling with thermostat.)*

Well I'll be. *(She looks at photo.)* Aw, isn't that just the sweetest thing.

**MARTIN.** What is it?

**ANGIE.** It's a letter. From Jose.

**MARTIN.** Who?

**ANGIE.** Jose. The new busboy in the clubhouse dining room. He simply has the biggest smile you've ever seen. A real charmer.

**MARTIN.** *(suspicious)* Oh? And just what is this 'real charmer' doing sending you letters, huh? A woman your age has to be careful when some Latin type starts flashing his teeth. He's only after one thing.

**ANGIE.** *(annoyed)* Oh and just what might that be?

**MARTIN.** What she has in the bank.

**ANGIE.** *(exasperated)* You are just impossible! Only for your information, it's not like that at all. If you really must know, one of the waitresses mentioned his little girl needed an operation on her legs. She'd never walk properly if she didn't have it. A real heartbreaking story. *(hotly)* So there!

**MARTIN.** What's any of that got to do with you?

**ANGIE.** Not that it's any of your business, but it was going to cost a fortune. I just felt so bad I slipped him a few dollars. To help out. Then I got a couple of the other girls at my table to chip in. It was nothing, really. Now he's sent me the nicest note saying she's had the operation, is doing well and thanking me for all my help. I'm…I'm kind of speechless. And look, here's a photo of his daughter. Isn't she just adorable?

*(She shows picture to him. He isn't particularly interested.)*

*(genuinely moved)*

**ANGIE.** It makes me feel good to think someone is actually grateful for something I've done.

*(MARTIN starts packing up his toolbox. ANGIE heads towards kitchen.)*

I am right this second going to put this picture on my refrigerator door.

*(ANGIE goes into kitchen. She appears moments later and resumes her Tai Chi. MARTIN is heading towards front door. Something suddenly occurs to her.)*

That's it!

*(MARTIN stops in his tracks.)*

**MARTIN.** That's what?

**ANGIE.** *(excited)* This is just what we've both been looking for.

**MARTIN.** We?

**ANGIE.** Yes. Have a seat.

*(She motions for him to take a seat. He puts his toolbox down on floor and goes over and sits on sofa. She paces room excitedly.)*

**ANGIE.** What do you and I have more than enough of?

**MARTIN.** *(facetiously)* Aches and pains.

**ANGIE.** No. Seriously.

**MARTIN.** Gas?

**ANGIE.** Martin!! *(dryly)* And speak for yourself. Well?

**MARTIN.** *(impatiently)* I don't know. What?

**ANGIE.** Money.

**MARTIN.** *(protesting)* Oh, I'm not so sure about that.

**ANGIE.** Come off it. You've got plenty. And Jerry left me very well provided for. You and I have everything we need and everything we'll ever need. Right?

MARTIN. *(grudgingly)* True.

ANGIE. And we both have loads of time on our hands. Why I just spend my days keeping busy with exercise classes, make-work projects and endless committees. But it's all so frivolous. Well, this is our chance. To make a difference. To do something meaningful. For people who have less. Like Jose.

MARTIN. What are you getting at?

ANGIE. That we extend a helping hand to those less fortunate.

MARTIN. *(disdainfully)* You mean charity work? Forget it! I'm not delivering meals to a bunch of old codgers. Standing around watching 'em gumming their food isn't exactly my idea of a life enhancing experience.

ANGIE. That's not what I'm talking about. We can put our money to work to help others.

MARTIN. Oh no! I'm not giving my dough to any rip off charity. They're all a bunch of con artists. Claiming the money is going to one thing – then spending it on something else completely. Like their own exorbitant salaries.

ANGIE. That's just it. We cut out the middlemen and give the money directly to the people involved. We find those in need and then help them ourselves. That way we know exactly where the funds are going. To folks right here, under our very over privileged noses.

*(*MARTIN *gets up to leave.)*

MARTIN. Do what you want with your money but you can forget about getting into my wallet. Most of 'em just need to get a job instead of looking for handouts.

*(*ANGIE *takes his arm and pulls him back down.)*

ANGIE. I'm talking about people with jobs who can barely make ends meet. A catastrophe or illness hits and they're destitute. Oh I hear the stories. From my manicurist. From the girl who works behind the deli counter at Blekman's. They tell me things. About people who have fallen on hard times.

(**MARTIN** *gets up.*)

**MARTIN**. You finished?

**ANGIE**. Yes.

**MARTIN**. Good. I'm going home. It's a hell of a lot cheaper over there.

**ANGIE**. Fine. Be like that. Only I'm telling you Martin, just now, with that letter, that's the best feeling I've had in years.

(**MARTIN** *heads towards front door. She stands in front of him to stop him.*)

Just answer this one question. What wonderful things are you doing with your money right now? Huh? How many times have you complained to me that your son only calls when the company you passed on to him needs more funds?

**MARTIN**. *(angry)* Don't remind me! To him I'm nothing more than a cash cow.

**ANGIE**. Bull!

**MARTIN**. *(taken aback)* What do you mean, bull?

**ANGIE**. Technically, you're a cash bull. *(forcefully)* So put a stop to it! Quit giving him the money and give it to people who'll appreciate it. My kids are no better. Every year I send my daughter and her husband gifts and checks for their birthdays. Not a peep out of them. And my Larry, he's even worse. I can't tell you how often I've lent him money. Then complete silence. Until he needs more.

**MARTIN**. Makes my blood boil. He doesn't have time for me now, but stands to get everything when I'm gone.

**ANGIE**. Exactly! After all their neglect they'll get a big reward at the end. And you'd better believe they'll have a field day.

**MARTIN**. And how! Blowing it on things like arugula. Whatever the hell that is. And their sun-dried tomatoes.

**ANGIE**. Or their extra-extra virgin olive oil. That makes me laugh. They only consider virginity a virtue when it comes to their salad dressing.

**MARTIN**. *(warming to the idea)* You know, you just might have something there. I kind of like the thought of screwing him out of his inheritance. Okay, Angie, you can count me in!

**ANGIE**. *(thrilled)* Oh Martin, that's wonderful!

*(She hugs* **MARTIN**. *She realizes that she's embraced him, is embarrassed and pulls away.)*

Sorry. I got carried away there. You're going to think I'm as bad as Vivian Hancock.

**MARTIN**. Good God, no one is as bad as her!

**ANGIE**. It's just that this is so exciting. You know what they say about money, don't you?

**MARTIN**. No, what?

**ANGIE**. It's like manure. It doesn't do any good unless you're spreading it around!

*(They both laugh.* **ANGIE** *rubs her hands gleefully.)*

So let's start spreading!

*(lights dim)*

## Scene Three

*(Lights rise on* **ANGIE**'s *living room several weeks later.
There are dozens of brochures scattered on the coffee table.*
**ANGIE** *is at desk typing on laptop. She finishes typing
and sits back.)*

**ANGIE.** *(to herself; satisfied)* Finished. *(She pushes a key.)* Send!
*(She stretches to relieve tension in her back.)*

*(Phone rings.* **ANGIE** *answers it.)*

*(into phone)*

Hello. … Oh hi, Judith. … No, you're not interrupting
anything. I just finished sending off an e-mail to my
broker. Who'd have imagined. A few weeks ago I wasn't
even on the information highway, now I'm speeding
along it at thousands of miles an hour. *(She laughs.)* …
Yes, that was quite the turnout for last night's meeting
at the clubhouse. My phone's been ringing off the hook
all morning. Seems everyone wants to contribute. It's
a shame you had to leave early. … Well, for a start, we
raised enough to buy that home dialysis machine for
Audrey's cleaning lady. Plus a Seeing Eye dog for Phil's
father-in-law. … Yes, Phil from the guard house. …
Oh, you'd better believe they're all legitimate causes.
Martin looks into each and every appeal that comes
to our attention. He's such a skeptic, nothing gets past
him. *(Her tone turns urgent.)* What's that? … *(hurriedly)*
I understand! GO!

*(***ANGIE** *hangs up. To herself.)* That poor woman. First her
dog loses bladder control – then her husband. Between
the two of them she never gets a moment's peace.

*(***ANGIE** *heaves a sigh. Phone rings.* **ANGIE** *answers it.)*

*(into phone)*

Hello. …. Hi Brenda, sorry I didn't get a chance to talk
to you last night. There were just so many people. …
Of course we still need money. I have a heartrending
case of a little boy desperately in need of a wheelchair.

And you can't even begin to imagine how much it will cost to have his house made accessible. *(businesslike)* So, how much can I put you down for? .... *(impatiently)* What's there to think about? You know perfectly well what will happen to your money if you leave it to your kids. They'll start by frittering it away on yet another trip to Tuscany. ... *(elated)* Ten thousand! Why that's marvelous. Remember to check out my blog. I've posted pictures of everyone we've helped so far, along with their letters of gratitude. Now I really have to dash. We'll talk again soon. Bye.

*(ANGIE hangs up. She goes into desk drawer and takes out her checkbook. She writes out a check and rips it out of book with a flourish. She gets up and looks around room.)*

ANGIE. *(to herself)* Now where did I leave my purse?

*(She spots purse on sofa. She picks it up, opens it and puts check inside. Just as she heads towards front door, MARTIN enters through it. He is totally transformed. He is well groomed and his clothes are neat and clean. He has a renewed vigor and his mood is upbeat. He carries a box of stationary.)*

Well look who's here. How are you this morning, Martin?

MARTIN. *(chipper)* On top of the world. I can't tell you how good it is to be alive! How about you, Angie?

ANGIE. I'm absolutely rushed off my feet and loving every second of it. *(She points to coffee table.)* Oh, before I forget, I received more brochures for all that accessibility equipment we're researching.

MARTIN. Great. We can go over them right now if you want.

ANGIE. No. Sorry I can't. I was just on my way out the door. You know how I've been looking for an apartment for the Peppler family?

MARTIN. Of course. I can hardly sleep nights thinking about them.

Their house burns down. There they are with six kids. No insurance. Nothing. All they got out with were the clothes on their backs. A crying shame.

**ANGIE.** *(brightly)* Well, as of right now, they have a place to live.

**MARTIN.** Hey, that's terrific!

**ANGIE.** Yes. I've found them an apartment. I'm just on my way over to give the landlord their deposit. *(She goes to exit, then stops.)* Oh, by the way, I almost forgot. You were magnificent last night.

**MARTIN.** *(slightly hurt)* I was wondering when you were going to say something. *(modestly)* Only I wouldn't say 'magnificent.' I will admit to being better than average. Considering I haven't done it in so long.

**ANGIE.** Well you could have fooled me. You just seemed so natural. So in control.

**MARTIN.** *(preening slightly)* You're embarrassing me. But keep going.

**ANGIE.** All in all it was quite the performance. Standing up there in front of all those people. Speaking so eloquently. I have absolutely the worst stage fright. I'd have died a thousand deaths. But they hung on ever word you said about the work we're doing.

**MARTIN.** What can I say? I used to make business presentations all the time. This was no different. It's all about getting people to fork over their moolah.

**ANGIE.** Well, I especially loved what you said about the Eskimos. How did it go again?

**MARTIN.** Let me think. Oh yeah. The Eskimos put their old people on ice floes and let them drift out to sea. Our kids have put us on beach chairs and are just waiting for us to go out with the tide.

**ANGIE.** Well it certainly did the trick. At eight o'clock this morning I got a call from Jack Rainer. He insisted on personally picking up the tab for Mrs. Halliday's hip replacement. He said it's something he can relate to because there is more titanium in him than in his golf bag.

**MARTIN.** *(impressed)* I must have been good. That old skinflint only puts his hand in his pocket to adjust himself.

*(They both laugh.)*

**ANGIE.** You obviously have the gift of the gab, Martin Wheeler. Or I should say gift of the grab. People have been selling off stocks and bonds and simply donating like mad. Myself included. As I tell everyone, it'll serve our families right. My big clincher for all the women is to remind them that the mother always gets blamed for everything. I mean, did you know that Barb's daughter hasn't spoken to her in years? All because she didn't have a clown at her birthday parties. She claims that's the reason she can't keep a man or hold down a job.

**MARTIN.** Tell Barb here's what she should do to really mess with the little witch's brain. Arrange to have a clown at her funeral. If the daughter shows up – it'll blow her mind completely!

*(They both laugh. She notices box he carries.)*

**ANGIE.** What's that?

**MARTIN.** *(excited)* It's a surprise. Close your eyes.

**ANGIE.** Oh Martin, please, I don't have time for games.

**MARTIN.** Just humor me. Close your eyes. You're going to be thrilled.

**ANGIE.** *(grudgingly)* Well, okay. But I hate surprises.

*(**ANGIE** put her purse down on sofa. She closes her eyes. **MARTIN** puts the box down on the coffee table, removes lid, takes out a sheet of paper and holds it up in front of her.)*

**MARTIN.** You can open them now.

*(**ANGIE** opens her eyes and looks at the paper. She is delighted.)*

**ANGIE.** Oh Martin, we got it!

**MARTIN.** That's right. We are now officially a non-profit foundation. With our very own letterhead. See! Right here in big, bold letters. *(He points at lettering across top.)* "The S.I.N. Foundation."

**ANGIE.** Which stands for, "Spending It Now." Oh and there's our catchy little slogan.

**MARTIN.** *(reading; proudly)* "Seniors Doing It Together. While We Still Can."

**ANGIE.** And look. *(reading letterhead)* "Co-founders, Angela J. Drayton and Martin B. Wheeler."

**MARTIN.** We are now full-fledged philanthropists. Bill and Melinda Gates, eat your hearts out! This means we can offer donors tax deductions, while the capital gains repercussions of the invested....

**ANGIE.** *(cutting him off)* That's all mumbo-jumbo to me. All I know is it gives me a warm feeling all over.

**MARTIN.** Same here. Who knew giving money away would actually be more fun than making it? But do you want to know the best part?

**ANGIE.** What?

**MARTIN.** *(pleased)* The widows aren't buzzing around me anymore. I was wondering why, then last night one of the fellas at the club tipped me off. *(pausing for effect)* They think I'm taken.

**ANGIE.** Taken?

**MARTIN.** Yes. By you.

**ANGIE.** ME!?

**MARTIN.** *(smugly)* Uh huh! Seems tongues have been wagging about all the time we spend together. Word is we're practically shacking up!

**ANGIE.** *(indignantly)* Why those dirty-minded, busybodies.

**MARTIN.** *(cheerfully)* Couldn't have worked out better if I'd thought of it myself. Not a banana bread or tuna casserole on my doorstep in ages. The neighborhood geriatric Lolitas have been laying off.
*(suddenly irked)* Except for that Vivian. And she's a hard nut to crack. She cornered me last night, told me she wants to make a sizeable contribution.

**ANGIE**. That's fabulous.

**MARTIN**. Not really. There was one condition.

**ANGIE**. Oh?

**MARTIN**. Yes. That I have dinner with her. Tonight.

**ANGIE**. Oh no.

**MARTIN**. Oh yes. And she said she's making my favorite. Meatloaf!

**ANGIE**. Did you accept?

**MARTIN**. Yes, blast her. She had me over a barrel. If it means more money for our Foundation, it's the sacrifice I have to make.

**ANGIE**. Now that IS dedication. Anyhow, I'd love to stay and sympathize with you, only I've got to rush so those poor people can get into their new apartment. *(She turns to leave. She suddenly stops.)* The only problem with all this fundraising is you haven't done a lick of work around here since we started. I hate to keep pestering you, Martin, but could you possibly fix my bedroom ceiling fan? That squeak is driving me mad!

**MARTIN**. Oh, right. I almost got around to it the other day but got sidetracked. I had my toolbox out and everything.

**ANGIE**. Yes, I know. You left it in the lanai. I've tripped over it twice already. *(anxiously)* Now I've really got to go. *(She heads toward front door. She stops and turns.)* Please, Martin, fix that ceiling fan. *(teasingly)* Or I'll be forced to make an announcement that it's all over between us. Then your widow friends will descend.

**MARTIN**. *(mock horror)* Oh no! Not that!

**ANGIE**. You've been warned. See you later.

*(She exits. **MARTIN** proudly holds up a sheet of letterhead and admires it. He suddenly remembers the fan. He places sheet of paper back in box and replaces cover.)*

**MARTIN**. *(to himself)* That's right, fan. Better get to it.

*(He goes into lanai and gets his toolbox. He then heads down hallway to bedrooms. The living room is empty*

*for a few moments. The front door opens and* **ANGIE***'s son,* **LARRY DRAYTON** *and his wife,* **TRACI DRAYTON** *enter. The couple is in their mid-thirties.* **LARRY** *is an arrogant, self-important fellow.* **TRACI** *is a self-absorbed fashionista.* **LARRY** *struggles with several designer suitcases while* **TRACI** *holds a large take-out coffee cup from which she constantly sips.* **LARRY** *drops the suitcases.)*

**LARRY**. Well, here we are in beautiful "I see dead people" Florida!

**TRACI**. You've said that a dozen times since we landed, Larry. It wasn't funny the first time.

**LARRY**. Yeah, well, what about, "Everyone down here is so old they should open a store called 'Bed Bath and Beyond the Grave?'" C'mon now, you've gotta admit THAT'S funny!

**TRACI**. *(completely disinterested)* You are so juvenile.

*(***LARRY*** sneers at her.* **TRACI** *looks around room.)*

One thing's for certain, before we move in here, this whole place has to be completely renovated.

**LARRY**. *(shushing her)* Sssh!! Jeez Traci, watch what you say!

**TRACI**. What are you worried about? You saw your mother drive away just as our cab pulled up. I wonder where she was going in such a rush that she didn't even notice her own son.

**LARRY**. Hey, it's not as if she was expecting us. We didn't even know we were coming until the last minute. And what is she thinking, leaving her door unlocked like that? Anyone could just walk in.

**TRACI**. Honestly, old people.

*(With her coffee cup in hand,* **TRACI** *walks around the room, appraising it.)*

First thing we have to do is put in hardwood floors. And this furniture will definitely have to go. It's all so…so… *(distastefully)* FLORIDA! *(She admires a lamp.)* Except for

this. It's so out of date it's now actually retro. I wonder
how much we could get for it on eBay?

**LARRY**. *(lowering his voice)* I said, keep your voice down.

**TRACI**. Why?

**LARRY**. Because this is still my mother's place. It's not ours.
YET!

**TRACI**. That's not the way you talk at home. Back there you
make out like we're moving in tomorrow. *(mimicking
him)* "The minute my Mom bites the dust I'm taking
early retirement and heading on down to her place.
Goodbye winter. So long work. Forever!"

**LARRY**. Yeah, well, she looked pretty spry just now. You
never know, she could be like her mom. She lived to
be ninety-seven.

**TRACI**. *(horrified)* Ninety-seven?! Now THAT'S what I call
child abuse.

*(**LARRY** walks around the room checking things out. He
trips over a suitcase and holds his back in pain.)*

**LARRY**. Hell, Traci, did you have to bring so damned much
luggage?
We're only staying long enough to find out what's
going on, then we're out of here.

**TRACI**. *(defensively)* I just brought the bare necessities.

**LARRY**. *(incredulous)* A whole suitcase filled with nothing
but shoes? It's like living with a centipede.

**TRACI**. You are so unfunny.

**LARRY**. I'll tell you what's unfunny. The amount of money
you spend on them.

**TRACI**. Well, if you made more, it wouldn't be such a big
deal. I keep telling you to ask for a raise. *(She waves her
hands in front of his face.)* Hello! Reality alert. You work
for your father-in-law. He has to give you one.

**LARRY**. Oh sure. Like I'm going to ask your dad for more
money after I lost that big account on him. Use your
head.

**TRACI**. *(peeved)* All I know is, thanks to you, not one of those shoes is open-toed.

**LARRY**. What?

**TRACI**. Well you were in such a hurry to get down here, I didn't have time for a pedicure. I'm telling you now, these toes will not be seen by anyone this entire trip!

*(**LARRY** looks exasperated.)*

Even worse, I didn't have a chance to get a bikini wax. No woman in her right mind goes south without first getting a bikini wax.

**LARRY**. *(wincing)* Traci!

**TRACI**. What? It's not as if I'm talking Brazilian.

**LARRY**. *(uncomfortable)* Sheesh! Can you just stop! That's not something a guy likes to think about. All that hot wax and then Rrrrrrp! *(He makes ripping motion and winces in pain.)*

**TRACI**. Oh please. Men are such babies. It's a known fact women are able to endure the pain of childbirth and hair removal. And while we're on the subject, your back could do with a good shearing.

**LARRY**. You are so annoying. Can't you see I have more important things on my mind right now?

**TRACI**. Well you wouldn't have, if you'd kept a better eye on your mother in the first place. But oh no. You wait until it's too late. After she's started selling off her investment envelope.

**LARRY**. Portfolio. Her investment portfolio. How many times do I have to tell you that?

**TRACI**. Well whatever it is, she's been cashing in stuff like there's no tomorrow.

**LARRY**. *(lowering his voice)* Traci, we're not supposed to know that. The only reason we do is because I play squash with her broker. He just happened to let it slip she's been divesting like mad lately. He asked if she was buying a boat or something. He said from the looks of it, it's got to be a pretty big one. My mother buying a boat! That's a laugh. She gets seasick at a seafood buffet.

(**TRACI** *begins snooping around room.*)

**TRACI**. Well then, where's all the money going? *(She looks at the computer on desk.)* Look. She's got a computer. Oh my gosh, maybe she's into internet gambling. You can lose a fortune that way.

**LARRY**. Naw. Betting's not her thing. Unless Texas Hold 'Em was a line dance, she couldn't care less.

**TRACI**. *(sulking)* Well then, you come up with something. Go ahead, genius!

**LARRY**. *(thinking)* Well, ah, I don't know. Computer. Internet. Hmm. First thing that comes to mind is porn. That's it. Maybe she's into porn.

**TRACI**. Pornography? Are you nuts?

**LARRY**. It's possible. That stuff can get really expensive.

**TRACI**. *(suspiciously)* Oh?

**LARRY**. *(defensively catching himself)* Er…ah…so I've heard. *(getting back into it)* Oh yeah, people can spend hours and hours poring over it. Downloading – no pun intended – any chance they get. In the middle of the night when their wife is asleep. At the office. Even on their handhelds while stuck in traffic. Let me tell you, some of those sites cost a pretty penny. It can really add up.

(**TRACI** *looks at him, suspiciously. He catches himself.*) Ah, again, so I've heard.

**TRACI**. *(dismissively)* No way. That's a guy thing. Women aren't interested in porn. The only way we get hot and bothered surfing the web is shopping on-line. But from the looks of it, she hasn't bought anything new around here in ages.

*(They continue snooping.* **TRACI** *suddenly thinks of something.)*

GOD!!

**LARRY**. *(startled)* What is it? What'd you find?

**TRACI**. Nothing.

**LARRY**. Then why'd you say "God?"

**TRACI**. Because maybe she's found religion. You know, one of those TV ministries where they get people to send in their life savings. Oh, that would just be the limit, seeing all our money going to some hypocritical preacher so he can live in luxury. *(with evangelical fervor)* "Praise the Lord – and send me money so I can visit the sick and needy in my brand new, top of the line Mercedes!"

**LARRY**. You're way off base. My mother isn't the gullible type who falls for that kind of stuff.

**TRACI**. You never know. They prey on lonely, elderly widows. Unless!

**LARRY**. What?

**TRACI**. Unless it's a man.

**LARRY**. *(dismissively)* Forget it. My mother isn't the kind of woman to have a boyfriend.

**TRACI**. For a start, thirteen year old girls have boyfriends. Women her age have *(emphasizing the word)* LOVERS! *(**LARRY** winces.)* You are in such denial. She's having an affair. I can just feel it in my bones. She is carrying on a torrid romance with some smarmy Casanova.

**LARRY**. Don't be ridiculous. And since when are you such an expert on affairs?

**TRACI**. Because I'm a woman of the world. I watch Dr. Phil. *(really getting into it)* She's feeling bored. One night out of loneliness and frustration she slips into a slinky, low cut little number. She goes out to a singles bar. She's just sitting there, sipping something with an umbrella in it.

**LARRY**. Traci, stop!

**TRACI**. No. Just listen! She looks like she's got a few bucks. Some over-tanned guy sidles up to her. His jet-black hair all slicked back. Wearing way too much gold jewelry. His shirt open to here. *(She indicates her navel.)* Before you know it, it's wham, bam, thank you…!

*(**LARRY** is uncomfortable hearing any of this and cuts her off.)*

**LARRY.** Hold it! Enough with the wham, bam, stuff. *(He cringes.)*

That's my mother you're talking about.

**TRACI.** Trust me, it's some sleazy, gigolo just out for what he can get. A little sweet talk, a couple of rolls in the hay and before you know it he's taking her to the cleaners.

**LARRY.** Can we just drop this entire conversation, huh? *(He holds his head in pain. He looks around.)* Let's just keep looking. See if we can find out what's going on before she gets back.

*(**TRACI** points to kitchen door.)*

**TRACI.** What's through there?

**LARRY.** Your guess is as good as mine.

*(**TRACI** goes into kitchen. **LARRY** heads out to lanai. A second later she sticks her head out the door.)*

**TRACI.** It's the kitchen.

*(She goes back into kitchen. She comes out moments later.)*

She obviously hasn't used the money to re-do anything in there. No granite counter tops. Not even a single stainless steel appliance. And, get this, floral wallpaper with matching curtains! *(She sticks her finger down her throat in mock gagging gesture. She then looks at floor.)* On second thought, imported Italian tiles would look stunning. *(She looks around for **LARRY**.)* Where are you?

**LARRY.** Here. Out back.

*(**TRACI** sees him and goes over to lanai. They both look out at view.)*

Get a load of that course. If I'd known this was here, I'd have been down a lot sooner. Once this is ours, I can just see myself out there working on my swing and living the good life. *(smugly)* Oh yeah, pretty soon the only commute I'll be making is from right back here to the clubhouse.

(**LARRY** *makes like he has a club in his hands and practices a few swings.* **TRACI** *points outside.*)

**TRACI.** *(concerned)* What's that over there?

**LARRY.** *(looking out; sarcastically)* Duh, I think it's called a tree!

(**TRACI** *punches him on shoulder.*)

**TRACI.** I know it's a tree. But what's it doing right there, blocking the sun where yours truly will be working on her year-round tan? That will definitely have to go!

**LARRY.** Yeah, well, we're forgetting why we're here. Let's not waste any more time.

(*They come out of lanai and start walking around living room. He spots the box of letterhead on coffee table and picks it up while she is busy snooping around desk.*)

Hold on. Here's something.

(**TRACI** *goes over to him.*)

**TRACI.** What is it?

**LARRY.** A box of stationary. *(He takes cover off. They both look inside box and their jaws drop.)* "The SIN Foundation." What the hell is that? (**LARRY** *takes sheet of paper out of box and reads from it.)* "Seniors Doing It Together. While We Still Can." *(flabbergasted)* Holy crap! This is REALLY bad.

**TRACI.** *(self-righteously)* You wouldn't believe she was fooling around with just one guy. Now it turns out she's involved in some kinky, pensioners sex cult. *(She takes the sheet of paper from him.)* Oh my GOD! Not only is she involved, she's one of the ringleaders. *(reading)* "Co-founders, Angela J. Drayton and Martin B. Wheeler."

**LARRY.** Who's he?

**TRACI.** Isn't it obvious? Some randy, Viagra-popping old stud!

(**TRACI** *picks up some of the brochures from coffee table. She looks through them, horrified.*) Ugh! This is just plain gross. Look! *(She hands brochure to* **LARRY**.*)* It's for crutches and canes.

**LARRY.** What are they getting up to with THOSE?!

**TRACI.** *(exasperated)* Do I have to spell it out for you? S&M!

(**LARRY** *grimaces. He looks at another brochure.*)

**LARRY.** This one's for grab bars and bed pulleys. What's she turned her bedroom into? A sexual gymnasium? *(He is so taken aback he plops down onto sofa.)* Oh Jesus!

**TRACI.** This is just so unbelievable. I thought 'senior moments' were supposed to be things like memory lapses and incontinence. Not multiple org…

**LARRY.** *(cutting her off)* TRACI!! *(mournfully)* This is all too friggin' much. I mean we are talking about a woman who won't even go into a store and ask for a three-way lightbulb because it sounds vaguely obscene!

(**MARTIN** *comes into living room from bedroom hallway. He sees two strangers in the home and approaches them aggressively.*)

**MARTIN.** Hey, hold on a minute. Who are you and what are you doing here?

(**LARRY** *gets up off of sofa.*)

**LARRY.** Never mind us, what the hell are you doing in my mother's house?

**MARTIN.** Angie's your mother?

**LARRY.** Yes, I'm Larry Drayton. Her son. Who are you?

(**MARTIN** *extends his hand to shake* **LARRY**'s. **LARRY** *doesn't hold his out.*)

**MARTIN.** I'm a friend of your mom's. A good friend. Name's Martin.
Martin Wheeler. (**LARRY** *and* **TRACI** *exchange looks.*) Funny, I don't remember her mentioning you coming down. I'd have remembered that.

**LARRY.** Yeah, I'm sure you would have.

**MARTIN.** She's a fine woman, your mother. So full of life. Always game for anything.

**LARRY.** *(mournfully to* **TRACI***)* Aw Jeez! I'd rather not hear about it.

*(***LARRY** *and* **TRACI** *grimace.* **MARTIN** *extends his hand to* **TRACI***.)*

**MARTIN.** And you must be his wife. Pleasure meeting you.

*(***TRACI** *limply shakes his hand then surreptitiously wipes it on her clothing.)*

**TRACI.** I'm Traci Drayton. That's Traci with an "i".

**MARTIN.** Well, I'm sure Angie will be pleased to see the two of you. She's just stepped out for a while. *(He gestures for them to sit.)* Have a seat. She should be back shortly.

*(***LARRY** *is upset to see the man there and refuses to sit.)*

**LARRY.** No, we'll stand. What I'd like to know is, what are YOU doing here?

**MARTIN.** Why I was just finishing up in your mother's bedroom. Doing what I can to help out a woman all on her own.

*(***LARRY** *and* **TRACI** *look at one another, their eyes widen.)*

I don't like to brag, but I am pretty good at what I do. The secret is taking your time and having the right equipment.

*(The couple look at one another in disgust.)*

**LARRY.** *(to* **TRACI***)* This is all FAR too much information.

*(***MARTIN** *heads towards front door.)*

**MARTIN.** At any rate, I was just heading back to my house.

**TRACI.** So you don't live here?

**MARTIN.** Here? Oh no. I live next door.

**LARRY.** *(sarcastically)* How convenient.

**MARTIN**. *(oblivious to* **LARRY***'s tone)* Yes, it is. But I'll be back in a flash. Just have to get something.

*(**MARTIN** exits. **TRACI** and **LARRY** look at one another.)*

**TRACI**. *(incredulous)* THAT'S lover boy?

**LARRY**. So much for the hot-blooded Romeo with his shirt open to here. *(He points to his navel.)* If it was, you'd see his truss! God, he's ancient.

**TRACI**. What could any woman possibly see in him? *(passionately)*

"Oooooh Martin, baby, I want to run my fingers through your eyebrows." *(shuddering)* Yuk.

**LARRY**. If he's anything to go by, what do they have on tap at their orgies? Formaldehyde?

**TRACI**. All I can say is, this is one cushy scene she's got going for herself. Setting him up in a love nest right next door. Which explains everything. Between him and all their paraphernalia, that's where the money's going!

**LARRY**. Oh this is bad. This is really bad! Something tells me this is going to take a lot of very expensive therapy to deal with.

**TRACI**. Yeah, well, I just hope she's practicing safe sex.

**LARRY**. TRACI!!

**TRACI**. I only meant making sure her life insurance is paid up. She could fall off one of those contraptions.

**LARRY**. *(shuddering)* Ugh! I feel so…so dirty. I could do with a good shower right now.

*(**ANGIE** enters through front door.)*

**ANGIE**. *(calling)* It's okay Martin, it's only me. I was half way there and realized I'd forgotten my purse. *(She notices the luggage on the floor. She turns and sees **LARRY** and **TRACI**. She is surprised.)* Larry! Traci! What on earth are you doing here?

*(She goes over and hugs **LARRY**.)* I can't tell you when I've been so surprised.

**LARRY**. *(meaningfully)* That makes two of us!

(**ANGIE** *stands back to get a good look at her son.*)

**ANGIE**. Let me take a good look. And Traci, darling, how wonderful to see you. *(She goes to* **TRACI** *who gives her a cold, awkward hug.)* But why didn't you let me know you were coming? I'd have been prepared.

**LARRY**. *(to* **TRACI**; *meaningfully)* I'll bet.

**TRACI**. Er...ah...it was just a last minute decision, Mother Drayton.

**LARRY**. Yeah, we thought we'd just pop in. Spend some quality time.

**ANGIE**. Oh don't give me that. I know you've come down to check up on me.

**LARRY**. *(guiltily)* We have?

**ANGIE**. *(teasingly)* Yes. To make sure your old Mom isn't playing too much Bingo and shuffleboard.

**LARRY**. *(relieved)* Oh yeah. Right.

**ANGIE**. Well, I'm just tickled pink to see you. How was your flight?

(*She notices luggage. She looks around.*) Where are they?

**LARRY**. Who?

**ANGIE**. Sam and Kimberly.

**LARRY**. They're not with us.

**ANGIE**. *(disappointed)* Oh, what a shame. I'd loved to have seen the kids. I can't even begin to imagine how much they've grown. Who's taking care of them?

**TRACI**. Christie. Our new nanny. We had to get rid of the old one because she just sat around all day drinking coffee and talking on her cell phone.

**LARRY**. *(sarcastically)* Yeah, and that's your job, right Honey?

**TRACI**. *(She shoots him a look.)* You're hysterical. A real comic. NOT!

**ANGIE**. It would have been wonderful for them to be here too. I'm so disappointed. *(cheerily)* But well, at least you're here. We'll have a terrific time. Now tell me, what have you been up to?

**LARRY**. Oh you know, same old, same old.

**ANGIE**. Well you'll be staying here, of course. That guest room has just been sitting there all these years waiting for you to show up.

*(***MARTIN*** enters through lanai, carrying a can of oil.)*

Martin, you'll never guess who's here. It's my son, Larry and his wife, Traci.

**MARTIN**. With an "i". *(***ANGIE*** looks confused.)* We've already met. *(He holds up can of oil.)* I just went home to get some WD–40 You know, for your little problem in the bedroom.

*(***LARRY*** and ***TRACI*** look mortified. ***MARTIN*** and ***ANGIE*** are oblivious to their discomfort.)*

*(to ***LARRY***)*

So, how long you here for?

**LARRY**. Why? Afraid we'll cramp your style?

**MARTIN**. Pardon?

*(***TRACI*** nudges ***LARRY*** to admonish him.)*

**TRACI**. Larry! *(to ***MARTIN***)* You'll have to excuse him. It's the jet lag.

**ANGIE**. *(confused)* Jet lag? It's a two hour flight. Well come on. Let's get you two unpacked then we'll go for lunch at the clubhouse. Just the three of us. We can catch up on everything. My treat.

*(***ANGIE*** picks up a suitcase and heads towards hallway to bedrooms.)*

Your room is just down here. You'll just simply love it, Traci. There's the most adorable floral wallpaper. With curtains and bedspread to match.

*(***TRACI*** rolls her eyes and looks anguished. ***LARRY*** and ***TRACI*** pick up a few pieces of luggage and follow ***ANGIE***.*

ANGIE *returns a moment later. She picks up stationary box and hands it to* MARTIN.)

*(frantically)*

ANGIE. Here, take this!

*(She rushes around gathering up brochures and hands them to him.)*

And these too. I don't want them to know what we're up to.

MARTIN. Oh yeah. Sure.

ANGIE. *(calling towards hallway)* Be right with you kids. I'll just see Martin out.

*(to* MARTIN*)* Remember now, not a word about "you know what."

*(*LARRY *appears in hallway. He overhears the following exchange.)*

MARTIN. Don't worry, I'll get rid of anything incriminating. And mum's the word. *(*MARTIN *taps the side of his nose.)*

ANGIE. Good. After all, what they don't know won't hurt them.

*(*MARTIN *heads toward front door with his arms full of stationary and brochures.* ANGIE *goes over and opens front door for him.)*

You know something?

MARTIN. What?

ANGIE. All this sneaking around almost makes me feel like a kid again.

MARTIN. *(delighted)* Yeah, me too!

*(*ANGIE *and* MARTIN *snicker.* LARRY *stands in hallway looking sickened.)*

*(lights dim)*

# ACT TWO

## Scene One

*(Lights rise on ANGIE's living room a few days later. Clothes and shopping bags are scattered everywhere. The room is empty. Doorbell rings. ANGIE comes rushing out of kitchen. She is wearing a sweater. She rushes towards front door.)*

**ANGIE.** *(in hushed voice)* I'm coming! Hold your horses, I'm coming.

*(ANGIE opens door. MARTIN enters. She puts a finger to her lips.)*

Sssh! Her majesty is still asleep.

**MARTIN.** *(astonished; loudly)* It's almost one!

*(ANGIE gestures for him to keep his voice down.)*

**ANGIE.** I know. But to her that's the crack of dawn. *(mimicking TRACI)* "I'm just not a morning person, Mother Drayton."

**MARTIN.** She's obviously not an afternoon person, either.

**ANGIE.** When the doorbell rang, I jumped a mile. Why didn't you just walk in, the way you usually do?

**MARTIN.** I didn't think it looked right with your family around.

Wouldn't want to give them the wrong impression about us.

**ANGIE.** That's sweet of you. Only I hardly think they're going to jump to any conclusions about the wild life I'm living. They know I'm not exactly the type who swings from chandeliers. If I ever got up on one it would be to dust.

*(She laughs at the ridiculousness of it all as she leads* **MARTIN** *to sofa. She picks up a few items of clothing to make room for him. She can't figure out where to put them so just dumps them onto another chair.)*

I give up. Have a seat.

*(***MARTIN*** sits. ***ANGIE*** gestures around room.)*

*(apologetically)*

You'll have to excuse the mess.

**MARTIN.** Looks like a hurricane hit the place.

**ANGIE.** It did. Hurricane Traci. With an "i". Actually, a hurricane would have been neater. You don't even want to know about their room. Towels just dropped on the floor. Clothes strewn everywhere. She picks nothing up. Not that my son is any better. God knows I didn't raise him like that.

*(She chuckles.)* Although I'm sure every mother in history has said that. I imagine even the mother of a serial killer says, "He may have killed all those people, but as God is my witness,he wasn't raised like that!"

*(She shivers and rubs her hands up and down her arms to warm herself.)*

**ANGIE.** And to top it all off, I'm freezing. I'll be lucky I don't catch pneumonia before they're gone.

**MARTIN.** Why? Isn't the air conditioning working properly? It should be after all I've...

*(***MARTIN*** goes to get up. ***ANGIE*** motions for him to stay seated.)*

**ANGIE.** No! Don't bother. It's working fine. It's just that they weren't here ten minutes before she started complaining about the heat. Next thing I know Larry's turned the air conditioning on full blast.

**MARTIN.** Why didn't you say something?

**ANGIE**. I did. Larry told me that's the way Traci likes it and that's the way it was going to stay. He said that if it was too cold for me, I should just put on a sweater!

**MARTIN**. *(irritated)* Well, that wouldn't have gone over too well with me.

**ANGIE**. It didn't with me, either. But what was I supposed to do?

They're only here for a week. I see them so rarely I didn't want to rock the boat. Although I must say, I was disappointed Larry didn't take my side.

**MARTIN**. If she can't take the heat, what's she doing down here?

**ANGIE**. That's what I keep asking myself. They say it's to see me. Only they've spent no time with me at all. They're either holed up in their room glued to the TV or out at the mall. Which is another thing that really steams me.

**MARTIN**. Why?

**ANGIE**. All they talk about is how much credit card debt they have. As if I'm supposed to do something about it. They claim they're maxed out. Stretched to the limit. But then all she does is shop. I'll bet even in her sleep she says, "I'll take it! I'll take it!"

**MARTIN**. *(disdainfully)* Aw, the whole bunch of them are the same. They want everything and they want it now!

**ANGIE**. You should hear her. *(mimicking* **TRACI***)* "Look at the divine earrings I bought, Mother Drayton." "Look at the silk blouse I bought. Isn't it divine, Mother Drayton?" The ultimate was yesterday when she said, "I just bought this. Tell me the truth. Does it make me look fat?" *(incredulous)* It was a handbag!

**MARTIN**. Sounds exactly like my son's second ex-wife. She's a real piece of work, that one. If I come back in another life, I want to be a dog.

**ANGIE**. Why?

**MARTIN**. So I could pee on her leg!

*(They both laugh.)*

**ANGIE**. Martin, you're just horrible. But seriously, the entire time they've been here I've had the strangest feeling they're checking out all my possessions. As if they're casing the joint before pulling off a big caper. *(She shrugs it off.)* Probably just my imagination. I'm just sorry I've been so distracted I haven't been able to concentrate on... *(She looks around and lowers her voice.)* ... The Foundation.

**MARTIN**. That's okay. I understand.

**ANGIE**. It's maddening to think about all those needy people out there. There are a million things to do. Only I don't dare make any calls in case they overhear.

*(**TRACI** appears in hallway. She has on shorty pajamas and a dressing gown. She is half-awake as she overhears the following conversation.)*

You have absolutely no idea how frustrated I am. I can't wait until they're gone and we can get back down to it. And once we do, you can bet I'm really going to make up for lost time.

**MARTIN**. What do you say we slip over to my place right now? We can do what we have to without them being any the wiser.

**ANGIE**. You know something, why not? We are talking about desperate people – who just can't wait.

*(**ANGIE** and **MARTIN** head towards front door. **MARTIN** rubs **ANGIE**'s arms with his hands.)*

**MARTIN**. First thing on the agenda is to get you out of that sweater and all warmed up!

*(**MARTIN** and **ANGIE** exit. **TRACI** stands rooted to the spot, grossed-out by what she thinks she's overheard.)*

**TRACI**. *(to herself)* Now THAT I did not need to hear first thing in the morning!

*(She takes her cell phone out of her dressing gown pocket and dials a number.)*

*(into phone)*

Christie! It's me. *(impatiently)* … No, I don't want to talk to the kids. Why would I want to do that? *(She looks at the phone as if the person on the other end is crazy.)* Have you picked up my dry cleaning? … *(irritated)* Well get a move on it, Christie. I'll need my black strapless as soon as I'm back. What's the use having a perfect tan if I can't show it off? … What do you mean that isn't in your job description?

Neither is watching our big screen, hi-definition, surround sound, plasma TV. So don't go giving me attitude because I can out attitude you in my sleep! And another thing…

*(**LARRY** enters through front door. He is wearing shorts, a T-shirt and sandals. He has a beach towel around his neck and is visibly upset.)*

**LARRY.** *(calling)* TRACI! Where the hell are you Traci?

*(He suddenly sees her.)*

Oh good, you're here.

**TRACI.** Sssh! Can't you see I'm on the phone?

**LARRY.** You're always on the phone. Hang up!

**TRACI.** *(protesting)* But…

**LARRY.** *(firmly)* I said hang up! NOW!

*(**TRACI** hangs up obediently without even saying goodbye.)*

**TRACI.** What's the matter? *(glaring at him)* This had better not be just another one of your lame jokes, like *(lowering her voice and mimicking him)* "Where do they buy their sweat pants down here? Old, Old, REALLY Old Navy!"

*(**LARRY** looks around room, frantically.)*

**LARRY.** Where is she?

**TRACI.** Who?

**LARRY.** My mother, who do you think? Is she around?

**TRACI**. No. She just went over to lover boy's. So she can, "get back down to it" because she's really, REALLY desperate! One thing's for certain, you take after your father because that woman obviously wants to do it ALL the time! Not just after her team wins a playoff!

**LARRY**. Yeah, well, that's where we've got it all wrong. They're not a pack of over-sexed fossils after all. Only what they're really up to is even worse. Much worse! I just found out what this S.I.N. Foundation actually is.

**TRACI**. *(anxiously)* So TELL me! What is it?

**LARRY**. I'm lying out there around the pool and these old biddies are yakking away. About the perils of fibre. Too much versus too little. Then I hear them say something about a foundation. My ears pick right up. *(incredulous)* Oh you are just so not going to believe this. It's incredible!

**TRACI**. *(frustrated)* So tell Me!!

**LARRY**. Turns out it's some kind of charity!

**TRACI**. Charity?

**LARRY**. Yes. *(unbelieving)* I can't believe this is happening to me!
(*He takes a breath.*) They're all chipping in big bucks to help people.

**TRACI**. *(incredulous)* Help people! With OUR money?!

**LARRY**. Yes.

**TRACI**. Larry, if you're just trying to get my goat, so help me…

**LARRY**. *(cutting her off)* I wouldn't kid about a thing like this! Remember those brochures for crutches and canes and things we saw when we first got here?

**TRACI**. *(revulsed)* Please, I still can't get the image out of my mind.

**LARRY**. Well those were actually for people who need crutches and canes! Can you believe it? Everyone in this complex is cashing in investments and raiding bank accounts to pay for all that junk. Bunch of demented do-gooders! All so they can blow their kids' inheritances.

**TRACI.** *(shocked)* WHAT? They said that?

**LARRY.** Yes! It's all a conspiracy. Against us!

**TRACI.** You're telling me we are the victims of some senility driven vendetta? That is just SO wrong!

**LARRY.** Tell me about it.

**TRACI.** *(stammering; flabbergasted)* But I...oh my GOD! This is just too.... I mean it's WAY beyond anything... *(composing herself)* Are you telling me that one day they're going to Early Bird Specials – eating dinner at four in the afternoon to save a dollar – then the very next day they're giving away fortunes? *(exasperated)* They're all off their rockers. The State bird of Florida is obviously a cuckoo!

**LARRY.** *(pacing agitatedly)* This has got to be my worst nightmare come true. And what really kills me is all the time she's just throwing money away – she only has basic cable. I am missing games because she's too tight-fisted to pay for the sports package! Infuriating!

*(In frustration, he picks up a pillow from sofa and pounds his fist into it.)*

**TRACI.** She is nothing but a selfish old woman. Hasn't she ever heard that charity begins at home? WE could use that money. This is really the limit, Larry. You have got to talk to her. NOW!

**LARRY.** I can't.

**TRACI.** Why not?

**LARRY.** You know my mother. You can't tell her anything. She'll just dig her heels in and do whatever she damned well wants. She won't listen to anyone. Least of all me.

**TRACI.** But she can't just keep giving it away. The money isn't going to last forever. You have to stop her!

**LARRY.** What can I do?

**TRACI.** I don't know!

*(Panicking,* **TRACI** *starts pounding him on the chest.)*

I don't know! But you have to act fast! While there's still something left.

*(***LARRY*** *grabs her arms to stop her from pummelling him.)*

**LARRY.** Calm down, Traci! Calm down!

**TRACI.** You calm down! Our future – everything we've ever dreamed of – is just slipping through our fingers! *(hysterically)* Do something Larry! Do SOMETHING!!

*(lights dim)*

## Scene Two

*(Lights rise on **ANGIE**'s living room the next afternoon. At rise the room is empty. It is still somewhat in disarray with clothing and shopping bags scattered around. **ANGIE** enters from kitchen with a book in one hand and a cup of tea in the other. She is wearing a sweater. She looks around at the mess in the room and shakes her head in disgust.)*

**ANGIE.** *(to herself)* Just three more days, Angie. Just three more LONG days.

*(**ANGIE** goes into the lanai and sits in chair under palm tree so that she is barely visible. She takes a sip of tea and opens her book. Just as she settles in, **TRACI** and **LARRY** enter through front door. **TRACI** is wearing sunglasses and a floppy hat, carrying the ubiquitous coffee cup.)*

**LARRY.** *(whispering)* Well, that was one hell of a crappy morning.

*(In background **ANGIE** gets up out of chair and takes a few steps towards living room to greet them.)*

We had to spend it making a bunch of frantic phone calls. All thanks to Lady Bountiful.

*(**ANGIE** suddenly stops in her tracks.)*

**TRACI.** You don't have to bother whispering. She's probably not home. I'll bet she's busy next door with Grandpa Moses. Working on their underhanded scheme to cheat us out of what is rightfully ours.

*(**ANGIE** backs up and sits down in chair. She picks up her book, opens it, folds it across her chest, closes her eyes and pretends to be asleep.)*

**LARRY.** He's the one who put her up to this. He's brainwashed her, that's what he's done. That...that liver-spotted Svengali. If I had my way I'd sue him for everything he's got for exerting undue influence over her.

*(TRACI takes off her hat and sunglasses and casually tosses them aside.)*

**TRACI.** You already talked to that lawyer about it. He told you to forget it. He said it would never stand up in court.

**LARRY.** *(frustrated)* Well, someone's put her up to this...this Mother Teresa act.

**TRACI.** At least he gave you some legal advice on what you can do to stop her. Okay, now go over it again, so I get it straight in my mind.

**LARRY.** *(irritated)* Every shoe Jimmy Choo ever made you can remember – right down to the tiniest detail. A few legal manoeuvres, you can't retain for two seconds.

**TRACI.** Don't start with me, Larry. Just tell me again and forget the sarcasm. Or that lawyer will be acting as MY divorce lawyer.

**LARRY.** Alright, just cool it. Here it goes again – nice and slow. This time, concentrate. He told me the only thing we can do is have her declared financially incompetent. Prove that she's mentally incapable of taking care of her assets. Then appoint a family member as her financial guardian. Namely me!

**TRACI.** And you've talked to your sister Susan. She's willing to go along with that. Right?

**LARRY.** You'd better believe it. She's just as concerned about the money vanishing into thin air. *(smugly)* Actually, this whole thing could work to our advantage. Yours and mine.

**TRACI.** I'm all for that. How?

**LARRY.** The money'll be locked up so tight Mom won't be able to spend a dime. I'll be in charge of it all! Which means instead of having to wait until something happens to her, we can get our hands on it now. When we can really use it.

**TRACI.** What about Susan and her bozo husband? Won't they object?

**LARRY**. No, because they're such schmucks they won't realize what's happened until it's too late. I've thought it all out. It's a piece of cake. Remember that plot of land on the lake back home that Mom owns?

**TRACI**. Are you kidding? I've had my heart set on it forever. We could build our dream home out there. I have such plans. Starting with tons of closet space. A home theatre. A pool with jacuzzi. Thirty-two jets.

**LARRY**. Well, we can build that house on it, right now.

**TRACI**. *(thrilled)* Larry! I can't believe this. It's too good to be true. *(She hugs him. Suddenly concerned.)* But how?

**LARRY**. Easy. We'll build it for Mom.

**TRACI**. *(disappointed)* Your Mom? That sucks!

**LARRY**. Wait, you haven't heard the whole plan. We only SAY it's for her. No one can object to us using her money to build a house for her, can they?

**TRACI**. No. I guess not. So go on.

**LARRY**. Then we move in with her. To… *(He makes air quotes.)* "take care of her."

**TRACI**. *(protesting)* Living under the same roof as your mother! In OUR new house. I don't think so.

**LARRY**. It's only for a short while. Who knows, her health could take a turn. Or, once she's there we say we feel she'd be better off in a home. Where she can be with other people her own age.

**TRACI**. Okay. Now it's starting to sound better. Only those places can be very expensive. Promise we don't put her anywhere that costs too much. Even if she is paying for it.

**LARRY**. Naturally. Anyhow, before Susan and Jerk Face realize what's happened, we're sitting pretty in our very own six bedroom, four car garage house. And it'll be too late for them to do anything about it.

**TRACI**. *(admiringly)* Oooh, you really have thought of everything. *(concerned)* The only problem is we have to prove she IS financially incompetent.

**LARRY**. That's why I've got that psychiatrist coming over any minute now. That Dr. Krapinsky I talked to over the phone. This guy'll check her out, then sign a declaration stating she's not capable of taking care of her own finances. Once we've got that in our hands, we start proceedings. *(He looks at his watch, agitated.)* I sure hope she's back soon. I don't want him to miss her.

**TRACI**. *(concerned)* Just one thing.

**LARRY**. What?

**TRACI**. Supposing she finds out what we're up to?

**LARRY**. Don't worry, she won't. I told this guy to dress casual and pretend he's a friend of mine. We're going to make like we're just having a chummy get-together. All the while he's going to be giving her the once over to confirm she's out of her mind. Face it, anyone giving away big bucks the way she is has to be totally out of her gourd!

**TRACI**. You are just so brilliant, Larry.

*(She wraps her arms around **LARRY**'s neck, amorously.)*

**LARRY**. *(boastfully)* Hey, what can I say? You've either got it, or you ain't!

*(**TRACI** takes his hand and leads him towards the bedroom.)*

**TRACI**. Well big boy, you've got it. *(excited)* Mmmm, this is just getting me so excited. How about we slip into the bedroom until he gets here? I just might have a little treat in store for you.

**LARRY**. Really?

**TRACI**. What would you say to one of my nice, relaxing neck rubs?

Just the way you like it, too. While you're watching poker on TV.

**LARRY**. Sounds great to me. *(rubbing his hands gleefully)* Honey, we are in the money!

*(**LARRY** and **TRACI** exit down hallway to bedroom.
**ANGIE** gets up out of chair and stands with her hands
on her hips, glaring furiously. She tip-toes out of house
through lanai. Doorbell rings. **LARRY** comes rushing
out from hallway adjusting his clothing. **TRACI** follows
him.)*

That must be him now. That's good. We'll have a
chance to talk before she gets back.

*(**LARRY** answers door. **DR. KRAPINSKY** enters. He is a
serious man in his mid-fifties. He is casually dressed.)*

Dr. Krapinsky?

**DR. KRAPINSKY.** Yes.

*(**LARRY** shakes his hand.)*

**LARRY.** Pleased to meet you, Doc.

*(**DR. KRAPINSKY** is obviously not pleased with such
familiarity.)*

**DR. KRAPINSKY.** *(correcting him)* That's Doctor! Even though
I am informally attired, I am still here in a professional
capacity.

**LARRY.** Oh yeah. Sure. Doctor. I'm Larry Drayton. We
talked on the phone. This is my wife, Traci.

**TRACI.** With an "i".

**DR. KRAPINSKY.** Pardon?

**TRACI.** That's Traci with an…

**LARRY.** *(cutting her off; impatiently)* Yeah, yeah. Whatever.
We don't have all day! Let's get down to business. She
could walk in any second now. Have a seat.

*(**LARRY** motions for **DR. KRAPINSKY** to take a seat.
**TRACI** is ticked off with him as they all sit.)*

**DR. KRAPINSKY.** Right. Now, from what I understand, your
concern is that your mother is acting irrationally.
Financially.

**TRACI.** I'll say. She's just giving money away, left, right and
center.

**LARRY**. To so-called 'worthy causes.'

**DR. KRAPINSKY**. Well, as I mentioned over the phone, that certainly doesn't automatically indicate abnormal fiduciary behavior. *(He gestures around room.)* Especially since she does appear to be a woman of some means.

**TRACI**. But we're talking large sums of money here, Doctor. Thousands are just disappearing. She's never done anything like that before. We've got to do something to stop her!

**LARRY**. Er...ah....for her own protection. You understand.

**DR. KRAPINSKY**. Yes, of course. *(meaningfully)* I understand perfectly. Only you must realize that to have someone declared incapable of controlling their own finances requires them to manifest severe character disorders. My observations will entail analyzing at least four different personality components. Psychiatric. Cognitive. Functional. Decision-making. All have to be met in order to arrive at a conclusion relevant to the medical and legal definitions.

*(**LARRY** and **TRACI** look at one another, not having understood a word.)*

**LARRY**. Yeah, sure. Just as long as that all proves she's, well, you know... *(He twirls his finger at side of his head.)*

**TRACI**. Crazy.

**LARRY**. Wacko.

**DR. KRAPINSKY**. *(appalled)* Those are hardly the terms I – or anyone with an ounce of intelligence – would use.

**TRACI**. *(oblivious to his put-down)* Because she is very definitely not all there. Do you know what I've actually caught her doing?

**DR. KRAPINSKY**. No. Tell me.

*(**TRACI** leans forward, conspiratorially.)*

**TRACI**. She buries coffee grounds. Under the tree outside. Every single day. *(She sits back in chair, her arms folded, resting her case.)* If that isn't proof, I don't know what is.

(**DR. KRAPINSKY** *looks at her as if she's from Mars.*)

**DR. KRAPINSKY**. Of what? The fact she might just perhaps be environmentally friendly? I'm afraid I'll reserve judgement until I have a little more to go on than that. I won't be able to make a final diagnosis until I have observed your mother for myself.

**LARRY**. Sure. Sure. We understand.

(**ANGIE** *enters through front door. The three rise.* **LARRY** *and* **TRACI** *are nervous.*)

Here she is now. *(as an aside to* **DR. KRAPINSKY***)* Now remember, we're old college buddies. Okay?

**DR. KRAPINSKY**. *(grudgingly)* Yes. I suppose so.

**LARRY**. *(to* **ANGIE***; as casually as possible)* Oh, hi Mom. How's it goin'?

**ANGIE**. Why fine. Just fine. (**ANGIE** *sees* **DR. KRAPINSKY**.) Well, well, who do we have here?

**LARRY**. Oh, ah, this is a good friend of mine. Er...ah *(searching for his first name)*

**DR. KRAPINSKY**. *(supplying his name)* Roger.

**LARRY**. Right. My good chum, Roger. Funniest thing just happened. We were out at the mall and who do we bump into but my old pal from college. Haven't seen each other in years.

**TRACI**. *(babbling nervously)* Isn't that amazing. Bumped right into him. Just goes to show you it's a small world. A really small world. A really, really small...

**LARRY**. *(cutting her off)* Okay, she gets that it's a small world.

(**ANGIE** *goes over to* **DR. KRAPINSKY** *and they shake hands.*)

**ANGIE**. It's a pleasure Roger. Always nice to meet one of my son's friends. *(pointedly)* Considering he has so few. Most of the time I don't even like him and I'm his mother. (**LARRY** *is taken aback.*) Although, if you don't mind my saying, Roger, you appear so much older than Larry. Or perhaps it's just that Larry looks so much younger because he's never put in a full day's work in his entire life.

(**LARRY** *and* **TRACI** *look confused.* **ANGIE** *turns to leave room.*)

Well now, I'll just leave you alone and you can catch up on old times. School cheers and all that.

(**LARRY** *frantically jumps up and stops her from leaving.*)

**LARRY.** NO! Wait! Don't go!

**ANGIE.** No?

(**LARRY** *catches himself and tries to act casual.*)

**LARRY.** Er...ah...no. Stay out here with us, Mom. We see so little of you. We can all just hang out together for a while.

**ANGIE.** Well, sure. I'm flattered. If you insist. (**ANGIE** *sits. There are a few moments of awkward silence.* **ANGIE** *finally breaks it.*) So Roger, what line of business are you in? Do you work for your father-in-law, like Larry does? Which means that no matter how inept you are, you can't get fired.

**LARRY.** *(offended)* Hey Mom! What kind of thing is that...?

**TRACI.** Mother Drayton! Really!

**ANGIE.** *(feigning innocence)* What is it? Did I say something wrong? Well, Roger, what do you do? Please tell me you're an exterminator.

**LARRY.** A what?

**ANGIE.** An exterminator.

**LARRY.** Why?

**ANGIE.** Because I have two real pests in my guest room I'd love to get rid of.

**LARRY.** Mother! What the...?

**ANGIE.** *(to Doctor; pressing)* So, what is it you do, Roger? Well?

**LARRY.** *(quickly)* He's...ah...in real estate.

**ANGIE.** Real estate. How interesting.

**DR. KRAPINSKY.** It is?

**ANGIE.** Yes. I'm thinking of selling this place. Maybe you could give me some advice.

**LARRY.** Selling?

**ANGIE.** Oh yes. It's far too big for me. I could put all the money from the sale to very good use.

*(**LARRY** and **TRACI** look meaningfully at **DR. KRAPINSKY**. **ANGIE** jumps up.)*

Gracious, where are my manners? Let me get you some refreshments. How about some lemonade? Would you like a glass, Roger?

**DR. KRAPINSKY.** Yes, lemonade would be fine. Thank you.

**ANGIE.** Good. I'll be back in a jiffy.

*(**ANGIE** goes into kitchen.)*

**LARRY.** *(to **DR. KRAPINSKY**; eagerly)* Well? What do you think?

**DR. KRAPINSKY.** She seems perfectly normal to me.

**LARRY.** *(disappointed)* Damn!

**DR. KRAPINSKY.** If anything, a little prone to speaking her mind. *(He glares at **LARRY**. Pointedly.)* Perhaps with good reason.

**LARRY.** *(oblivious to the insult)* Yeah, I don't know where all that came from. *(hopefully)* Although just saying whatever comes into your head, well, isn't that a bit nutty?

**DR. KRAPINSKY.** Well, yes, loss of self-censoring mechanism can be one of the first signs of dementia.

**LARRY.** *(to **TRACI**; elated)* Hear that, Hon! *(He high fives her.)* Give me five!

*(**DR. KRAPINSKY** looks disgusted. **ANGIE** returns carrying a tray with a glass pitcher and four glasses on it. In the pitcher are several lemons. She puts tray down on coffee table. **LARRY**, **TRACI** and **DR. KRAPINSKY** all look at it in astonishment.)*

ANGIE. There we go. Nothing like a glass of nice, refreshing lemonade. Just help yourselves.

*(They all sit staring at the pitcher.* LARRY *finally breaks the silence.)*

LARRY. Er, ah, haven't you forgotten something, Mother?

ANGIE. Have I? *(She looks at pitcher, then laughs.)* Well, for the love of Pete, so I have. CRAZY me! Excuse me for one second.

*(She gets up and taking pitcher with her goes back into kitchen.)*

LARRY. *(pleased)* Now that's more like it. You taking all this in, Doc?

*(DR. KRAPINSKY glares at LARRY. He corrects himself.)* I mean Doctor.

DR. KRAPINSKY. Well, it certainly is eccentric behavior. But anyone can make a mistake. I make them myself from time to time.

*(archly)* Like making house calls!

*(ANGIE comes out of kitchen with the pitcher with lemons still in it. She carries a sugar bowl in other hand. She puts pitcher down on coffee table.)*

ANGIE. How silly of me. Honestly, I don't know where my mind is lately. I forgot the sugar.

*(She pours the bowl of sugar into the pitcher.* LARRY *and* TRACI *are agog.* LARRY *grins and rubs his hands gleefully. This is all exactly what he wants* DR. KRAPINSKY *to witness. Doorbell rings.)*

Now who in the world can that be? I'm not expecting anyone.

*(She goes over and answers door. It is* MARTIN.*)*

Ah, Martin. Good to see you.

*(MARTIN looks around.)*

MARTIN. Oh sorry, I didn't know you had company. I'll come back later.

**ANGIE.** Don't be ridiculous. Come right in. The more the merrier.

(**MARTIN** *enters.* **LARRY** *isn't pleased at the interruption.* **ANGIE** *gestures towards* **DR. KRAPINSKY.**)

Martin, I'd like you to meet… *(to* **DR. KRAPINSKY***)* … I'm sorry, who are you again? I know you told me but it seems to have slipped my mind.

**DR. KRAPINSKY.** I'm Larry's friend, Roger.

**ANGIE.** That's right. Martin, this is Larry's friend Roger. *(to* **DR. KRAPINSKY***)* Who's Larry?

**LARRY.** That's me. Your son, Larry.

(**ANGIE** *looks confused.*)

**ANGIE.** You are? Oh. *(to* **TRACI***)* Then you must be my daughter, Karen.

**LARRY.** No, your daughter's name is Susan. *(to* **DR. KRAPINSKY,** *pointedly with raised eyebrows)* Her daughter's name is Susan. *(to* **ANGIE***)* This isn't Susan, Mom. It's my wife, Traci.

**ANGIE.** You're married?

**LARRY.** *(patiently)* Yes, Ma.

**ANGIE.** I hope not to that horrid clothes-horse with absolutely no sense of humor you were dating.

**TRACI.** *(to* **LARRY***; insulted)* Did you hear what she said about me? Are you just going to let her get away with that?

**LARRY.** *(to* **TRACI,** *under his breath)* Quiet! Can't you see this is all working in our favor?

**ANGIE.** *(to* **MARTIN***)* So, Martin, what can I do for you?

**MARTIN.** You told me to drop by. You said you had something for me.

**ANGIE.** I did? Now what could it have been? My brain is like a sieve lately. *(thinking a moment)* Oh yes, I remember. *(She goes over to desk, opens drawer and takes out her checkbook.)* I wanted to give you a check. *(to others)* You just talk amongst yourselves. Reminisce about the good old days at that outrageously expensive college Larry flunked out of.

(**LARRY** *looks peeved.* **ANGIE** *writes out a check, rips it out of checkbook and hands it to* **MARTIN**.)

There. That's for being the best neighbor in the whole wide world.

(**MARTIN** *takes check and reads it.*)

**MARTIN**. *(pleased)* Say, that's quite generous of you, Angie. One million dollars!

**LARRY**. *(apoplectic)* A MILLION bucks! Ma, are you insane? You can't give him that. For a start, you don't have that kind of money.

**ANGIE**. What's the matter? Oh I get it, you're jealous. You want one too. Why didn't you just say so? *(She goes back to desk and begins to write another check.)*

**LARRY**. But Ma, you can't just give people checks for a million bucks!

**ANGIE**. You're right.

**LARRY**. *(relieved)* Thank God.

**ANGIE**. Of course not. What was I thinking? You're my son. My very own flesh and blood. I'll make yours out for two million.

(*She writes check, rips it out of book and hands it to* **LARRY**.) There you go, dear. *(She turns to* **DR. KRAPINSKY**.)

What about you? Let me give you something. I insist!

**DR. KRAPINSKY**. *(standing up)* No thanks. That won't be necessary. I have everything I need. In fact, more than I need.

(**LARRY** *looks pleased. He hands his check to* **TRACI** *then sees* **DR. KRAPINSKY** *to the door.*)

**LARRY**. Yeah, uh, well good bumping into you, old pal. *(He pats* **DR. KRAPINSKY** *on shoulder.)* Now that we've reconnected, we ought to stay in touch. You've got my number, right?

**DR. KRAPINSKY.** *(meaningfully)* Oh, I have your number alright.

**LARRY.** *(oblivious to the Doctor's tone)* Good. Good. Hope to hear from you soon.

*(LARRY winks conspiratorially at DR. KRAPINSKY.)*

**DR. KRAPINSKY.** Don't worry, you will. My bill will be in the mail first thing tomorrow.

**ANGIE.** Bill? What's that about a bill?

**LARRY.** *(flustered)* That's er… Bill, another buddy of ours. We all used to hang out together. That's it, good old Bill. What a character.

*(LARRY tries to usher DR. KRAPINSKY out the door.)* Be seeing you, Rog.

**DR. KRAPINSKY.** *(to LARRY)* Just so you know, my report will indicate that your mother is completely compos mentis.

*(LARRY looks at him blankly.)*

**LARRY.** *(expectantly)* Uh huh? And that means what exactly? *(eagerly)* She's nutty as a fruitcake?

**DR. KRAPINSKY.** No. It means she is possibly the sanest person in this room. Myself included. *(He bows politely to ANGIE.)* Very nice meeting you, Mrs. Drayton. I only wish it could have been under more pleasant circumstances.

**ANGIE.** How kind of you. And I agree. Goodbye, doctor.

*(LARRY stares open mouthed at his mother.)*

**LARRY.** Did you say doctor?

**ANGIE.** Yes. You heard me. Doctor!

*(DR. KRAPINSKY exits. LARRY calls after him.)*

**LARRY.** *(protesting)* Hey, wait a minute. What do you mean? You just saw what went on here. The lemons. The checks. The…

*(TRACI is looking at check and suddenly lets out a moan.)*

**TRACI.** Oh my God!!

**LARRY.** What is it?

(**TRACI** *holds up check.*)

**TRACI.** Did you…did you read this?

**LARRY.** Yes. It's a check for two million bucks. It's more than enough proof that…

**TRACI.** *(cutting him off)* Look at the signature! Just look how she signed it.

**LARRY.** What are you talking about? Give me that!

(**LARRY** *grabs check from her and looks at it. His eyes widen.*)

Holy shit! *(flabbergasted, he reads aloud)* "Mother Teresa!"

(**ANGIE** *takes check from* **MARTIN.**)

**ANGIE.** Yes, and you'll notice that this one is signed, "Lady Bountiful."

(**LARRY** *and* **TRACI** *suddenly realize the jig is up.* **LARRY** *slinks down into a chair.*)

**LARRY.** Oh Christ!

**TRACI.** Oh my God!

**ANGIE.** *(to* **LARRY,** *angry)* You are so busted, mister! Bringing a psychiatrist into my home. Into my own living room!

**LARRY.** You knew? You knew all along?

**ANGIE.** Oh you'd better believe I did. Trying to pass him off as your friend so he can observe me. Hoping to convince me I've lost my marbles so you can get your hands on my money!

All I can say is, you have really done it this time. This is the absolute limit! *(turning on* **TRACI***)* And you, you were right in there egging him on! It's despicable!

**LARRY.** Hold on Mom. I… I can explain everything. We were only doing this for your own good.

**ANGIE.** Don't give me that load of rubbish! *(pointing to lanai.)* I was right back there and heard every word out of your scheming mouths.

**LARRY**. *(accusingly)* You were eavesdropping on us? *(self-righteously)* That was a private conversation between a husband and his wife.

**ANGIE**. Don't go trying to turn the tables on me, young man! You've finally shown your true colors!

**LARRY**. *(turning on* **TRACI***; mimicking her)* "You don't have to bother whispering. She's never home. She's always busy next door with Grandpa Moses." Miss Know-It-All! NOW look what you've done!

**TRACI**. ME? Don't try and pin this on ME!

**ANGIE**. *(furious)* Just shut up, the both of you! *(to* **LARRY***)* You ought to be ashamed of yourself, dragging your sister into this whole sordid mess. I'll deal with her later. I'm just as furious with her. Meanwhile, I'm going to take care of you two right now. Conspiring to snatch everything out from under my nose so that this one – *(She points to* **TRACI***.)* – can have more closet space. God only knows why. She never hangs anything up!

*(to* **LARRY***)* I've suspected it all along, but now you've really proven to me you are a shiftless, greedy, bloodless creature! And I'm humiliated to call you my son!

**MARTIN**. *(embarrassed)* I… I think I'd better leave. This is a family matter.

**ANGIE**. Yes, perhaps you'd better. I'm pretty embarrassed about what just went on here. I don't want to air any more of our dirty laundry in public. Although not a bad little acting job we did there, right Martin? We really should think seriously about joining a local theatre group. Only we didn't have the psychiatrist fooled for a second. But we did have these two practically jumping for joy thinking they'd hit the jackpot!

**MARTIN**. I'll be outside. If you need me, just call.

**ANGIE**. Thanks. I will.

*(***MARTIN*** exits through lanai. ***ANGIE*** takes a moment to calm herself. She then turns on ***LARRY***.)*

You can't even begin to imagine how thrilled I was when I thought you'd just dropped in on me, out of the blue. I thought you actually wanted to see me. That you genuinely wanted to spend some time with your mother. *(She laughs bitterly.)* Ha, I should have known better. When I had my gall bladder operation last spring, did I hear from you? Oh no. No flowers. No get well card. Not so much as a phone call. But find out I'm giving away some of what you consider to be your money – you're down here in a flash. Then when you do get here, are you happy that I have a life of my own? Were you pleased that I have my health and all my faculties? Just the opposite, right? You were actually disappointed that I don't have Post-It Notes all over the place, reminding me to do things – the way some of the people down here have. Notes that say, "turn off stove," "lock door," "put out cat." And they don't even have a cat! No, you couldn't wait to prove I have a screw loose. So you could get your grubby paws on my money. And then put me in a home.

**LARRY.** *(defensively)* Not so much a home as a retirement village. It would have all the best of everything. You'd have round the clock care and…

**ANGIE.** *(cutting him off)* Don't give me that! *(despondently)* In a way, I almost wish I had lost my mind. Then I wouldn't be aware of what actually went on here today.

*(**LARRY** stands.)*

**LARRY.** *(meekly)* Ma, I know this looks bad, but just give me a chance to…

**TRACI.** Yes, we…

**ANGIE.** *(cutting them both off)* Just sit down!

*(She points at sofa. **LARRY** obediently sits.)*

There are some things I can finally get off my chest. Starting with how you never gave your children a chance to know their grandmother. Take your trip to Disney World. Would it have killed you to have visited me while you were down here? Or, God forbid, you might even have invited me to join you. I'd have been there in an instant. Well, answer me!

**LARRY.** *(weakly)* We never thought.

**ANGIE.** That's just it. You never once thought about me. Period. Unless you needed something. Oh, then you could call, alright. A mortgage on your house. Loans I'm still waiting for you to even make a gesture towards paying off. When you needed those you weren't too busy to get in touch. And now...now I see that you couldn't even wait to get me out of the way altogether with this incompetency fiasco.

**TRACI.** We had to do something. That money was just going to a bunch of strangers.

**ANGIE.** *(incensed)* I'd rather give it to perfect strangers who are truly needy and appreciative – than the likes of you. Oh, I was out of my mind, alright. For ever thinking you were interested in me for anything other than what you could get!

Well, I have come to my senses. You won't be seeing a red cent from me, ever again. The gravy train has just pulled out of the station. *(She heaves a deep sigh. Directly to **LARRY**.)* What really bothers me most is the fact that you, of all people, tried to take advantage of me. You're my son. You're supposed to be the one who protects me. When you get older, you expect to be ripped off by aluminum siding salesmen and tele-marketers. But your own child! It's...it's unforgiveable!

*(**ANGIE** goes over to thermostat and turns air conditioner off with a grand gesture.)*

And THAT is how I like it in MY home! *(calmly)* I am now going out. I'll be back in a half hour. When I return I want the two of you out of here. Gone! I don't want to set eyes on you ever again! Understand?

**TRACI.** *(protesting)* But Mother Drayton, our flight home isn't for another three days. Where will we stay?

ANGIE. In a hotel. God only knows you've treated this place like one. Now start packing because Hotel Angie is closing in… *(She looks at her watch.)* …exactly twenty-nine minutes. I suggest the first thing you do is call a cab on that cell phone that's glued to your ear twenty-four hours a day. *(She points at clothing scattered around room.)* You heard me. Get going! Starting with all this! *(She looks at her watch again.)* I'm counting.

*(LARRY and TRACI rush around collecting their belongings. As they head towards the bedroom, ANGIE stops them.)*

No. Hold it! Wait!

*(They both stop in their tracks, hopeful of a reprieve.)*

LARRY. *(expectantly)* Yes?

ANGIE. One last thing.

TRACI. What? What is it, Mother Drayton?

*(ANGIE cringes at the sound of "Mother Drayton.")*

ANGIE. It's about that piece of land on the lake you've coveted so much.

LARRY. *(hopefully)* Yes? What about it?

ANGIE. I always planned on giving it to you.

LARRY. *(optimistically)* You have? Wow! That's just great. We could really…

ANGIE. *(cutting him off)* In the not too distant future, actually. Only the more I think about it, the more I realize what a perfect setting it would make as a camp for special needs children. Consider it your donation to a more than worthy cause!

*(LARRY and TRACI are upset. TRACI whacks LARRY over the shoulder with one of the shopping bags.)*

TRACI. You and your bright ideas! *(mimicking LARRY)* "We'll just get her declared incompetent. *(She snaps her fingers.)* It's a piece of cake." *(exasperated)* You're the one who's incompetent!

LARRY. Aw, give me a break! You're never happy. Always wanting more and more and more. Manolo this. Louis Vuitton, that.

TRACI. And what about you? You just...

(**TRACI** and **LARRY** *continue blaming each other as they exit down hallway to bedrooms.* **ANGIE** *stands for a moment and heaves a deep sigh. She then goes over to lanai and calls to* **MARTIN***.*)

ANGIE. Martin! You can come in now, Martin.

(**MARTIN** *enters.*)

MARTIN. *(concerned)* Are you okay?

ANGIE. No. I've just made the hardest decision I've ever had to make in my entire life. But...but I know it's the right one. I've told them to get out of my life, forever.

MARTIN. Angie, I'm so sorry.

ANGIE. I... I never thought my heart could ever be so broken. *(bravely, pulling herself together)* Well, I guess that's that. I've told you enough times, life goes on. So I'd better start practicing what I've been preaching. Tomorrow you and I are going to get back to The Foundation – with a vengeance. *(She suddenly weakens.)* Only now, I... I think you'd better help me over to your place.

(**MARTIN** *puts his arms around her shoulders and leads her off through lanai.*)

*(lights dim)*

## Scene Three

*(Lights rise on* **ANGIE***'s living room several months later.* **MARTIN** *is alone in the room. He wears a suit with a boutonniere in his lapel. He paces nervously then goes towards bedroom hallway and calls.)*

**MARTIN**. Angie, what the devil is keeping you?

*(***MARTIN** *anxiously goes over to desk and pulls out drawers to see that they slide easily. He checks his watch then goes over to bedroom hallway and calls again.)*

*(impatiently)* We're supposed to be at City Hall at ten sharp.

*(He goes over to thermostat, fiddles with it. He can find nothing else to keep himself occupied and looks towards hallway, exasperated. He then begins adjusting his tie and brushing his jacket with his hand.* **ANGIE** *finally enters from bedroom hallway, somewhat flustered. She is dressed for a wedding. Her ensemble includes a hat and corsage. She carries a hanky.)*

**ANGIE**. I'm sorry. I almost forgot a hanky. *(She tucks hanky into her sleeve.)* I just know I'll cry. Even though I'm wearing water-proof mascara, I'll end up looking like a raccoon by the end of the ceremony.

*(***ANGIE** *stands and poses for* **MARTIN***.)*

Well? How do I look?

**MARTIN**. *(impressed)* Why Angie, you look sensational.

**ANGIE**. *(pleased)* Thank you.

*(***ANGIE** *gives a model turn, showing off the outfit.)*

This is a big day. I wanted to look my very best.

**MARTIN**. That you do, in spades.

*(***ANGIE** *stands back and takes a long look at* **MARTIN***.)*

**ANGIE**. As for you, well, I must say, you look very handsome. May I kiss the groom?

**MARTIN**. You most certainly may.

(**ANGIE** *kisses* **MARTIN** *on the cheek. She fans herself with her hand.*)

**ANGIE.** Honestly, I'm so nervous you'd think I was getting married. Instead of you and Vivian. I still can't get over it. You marrying Vivian Hancock. You sly devil. Why you could have knocked me over with a feather when you started seeing her so regularly. Especially after all the terrible things you used to say about her.

**MARTIN.** *(sheepishly)* I was a little hard on her. *(joking, to cover his embarrassment)* What can I say, huh? Her shrimp casserole gave me cramps so bad, I figured while I was down on my knees, I might as well propose!

**ANGIE.** Oh Martin, you're incorrigible! Well, she's a lucky lady. I couldn't be happier for the two of you.

**MARTIN.** *(seriously)* You're not just saying that are you? You and me – we have a long history together. I'll never forget how you were there for me after Peggy died.

**ANGIE.** *(soberly)* Yes, and you saw me through all the troubles with my children. *(cheering up)* But I told you ages ago, I don't need a man in my life. You can rest assured that if I was looking for one, I'd have snapped you up long ago. Besides, I have my new "chosen" family now. All the people you and I have helped. People who are truly concerned about me. Not just out for what they can get. Which reminds me, I've been asked to be godmother to the Peppler's new baby.

**MARTIN.** Congratulations, Angie.

**ANGIE.** Their seventh. They simply love their new apartment and get this, they call me every morning to see how I am.

**MARTIN.** Well, that's a switch.

**ANGIE.** So don't worry about me, Martin. I couldn't be happier. *(warmly)* And I just know you and Viv are going to be terribly happy together.

**MARTIN.** Me too. If only I can keep her out of the kitchen.

**ANGIE.** *(teasing)* So obviously the way to a man's heart ISN'T through his stomach. *(They both laugh.)* Well, she's a lucky lady. And it's not as if we'll never see each other again. The two of you will be living right next door. You and I will continue working together on our Foundation. Not much will change. But if I really need you, I'm sure Vivian won't mind sharing you from time to time.

(**ANGIE** *goes over and points to wall above desk.*)

And the first job I have for you is to hang my citation. Right here. *(amazed)* Just imagine, in a short while you and I are actually receiving commendations from the Mayor.

(**MARTIN** *takes piece of paper from his pocket and unfolds it.*)

MARTIN. I still can't believe. That's why I carry the official proclamation around with me. So I can see it in black and white. *(He clears his throat and reads very formally.)* "In recognition of their philanthropic efforts on behalf of the Spending It Now Foundation, Angela J. Drayton and Martin B. Wheeler have been chosen Citizens of the Year." *(He folds paper and puts it back in pocket.)* Turns out we weren't a couple of useless old fogies after all.

ANGIE. Especially you. You're still sharp as a tack – coordinating everything so that you get married right after our citation ceremony.

MARTIN. The way I looked at it, we're already at the City Hall, why not kill two birds with one stone?

(**MARTIN** *checks his watch.*)

Speaking of which, we'd better get a move on.

(*He takes her arm and leads her to front door.*)

ANGIE. Right. *(pre-occupied)* Only I can't help feeling there's something I'm forgetting. *(She suddenly stops, remembering.)* Of course!

(**ANGIE** *heads towards kitchen.*)

This won't take a second.

*(ANGIE goes into kitchen. MARTIN stands looking frustrated. A second later ANGIE comes out of kitchen carrying the spade and coffee filter. ANGIE exits through lanai. MARTIN calls after her.)*

MARTIN. Vivian's going to think I've left her standing at the altar.

*(ANGIE rushes back into living room, excited.)*

ANGIE. I don't believe it! I just don't believe it!

MARTIN. What?

*(ANGIE puts spade and filter down on coffee table and takes his arm.)*

ANGIE. Quick. Come with me!

MARTIN. This had better be good, Angie. It's practically cutting into my honeymoon time!

*(ANGIE leads MARTIN out lanai doors. They return a moment later. ANGIE carries an orange.)*

ANGIE. I've been so busy lately, I'd forgotten all about my tree. Never had a single orange on it, but now it's just bursting with them.

MARTIN. *(pleased)* If that isn't a good omen, I don't know what is.

*(ANGIE carefully sets the orange down on coffee table and proudly stands back to admire it.)*

ANGIE. The only problem is, now I don't know whether to squeeze it or bronze it.

*(They laugh. MARTIN checks his watch.)*

MARTIN. Meanwhile, the Mayor awaits. Shall we?

*(MARTIN holds out his arm. She takes it.)*

ANGIE. We've certainly come a long way since the days we had our little talks about how depressed and lonely you were.

MARTIN. I believe the word you muttered under your breathe was 'cantankerous.'

**ANGIE.** *(admonished)* I'm afraid so. And I was just keeping busy, for the sake of being busy. *(proudly)* Well, look at us now! *(thinking)* I just thought of something.

**MARTIN.** *(impatiently)* What NOW, Angie?

**ANGIE.** What do we do for an encore?!

*(They both laugh as arm in arm they walk out front door.)*

*(curtain)*

CPSIA information can be obtained at www.ICGtesting.com
Printed in the USA
LVOW08s2356310315

432821LV00012B/172/P

9 780573 702532